CW01669310

It was a nightmare society – a world of the 'cubs' – rebel hipsters drugged to a point of frenzy . . . of a vast underwater city gradually collapsing under the pressures of the sea . . . of an ice hell in polar regions where criminals were sent to survive if they could . . . of a desert inhabited by psychotic savages.

It was a world where there was little beauty and no peace . . . where man, condemned to a short lifespan, fought against his own terror and dreamed of Sanctuary . . .

William F. Nolan
and
George Clayton Johnson

Logan's Run

CORGI BOOKS
A DIVISION OF TRANSWORLD PUBLISHERS LTD

LOGAN'S RUN

A CORGI BOOK 0 552 10266 0

Originally published in Great Britain
by Victor Gollancz Limited

PRINTING HISTORY
Gollancz edition published 1969
Corgi edition published 1970
Corgi edition reissued 1976
Corgi edition reissued 1976

This book is set in 10/11pt Plantin

Corgi Books are published by Transworld Publishers Ltd.,
Century House, 61–63 Uxbridge Road,
Ealing, London, W.5.
Made and printed in Great Britain by
Hunt Barnard Printing Ltd., Aylesbury, Bucks.

TO ALL THE WILD FRIENDS WE GREW UP WITH—
and who were with us when we wrote this book:

To Frankenstein and Mickey Mouse
To Jack, Doc and Reggie and The Temple of the Vampires
To Fu Manchu, Long John Silver, Tom Mix and Buck Jones
To The Iliad and The Odyssey, Superman and The Green Hornet
To Jack Armstrong, the All-American Boy, and
The Hunchback of Notre Dame
To Gunga Din, King Kong and The Land of Oz
To Mr. Hyde and The Phantom of the Opera
To The Sea Wolf, Captain Nemo and The Great White Whale
To Batman and Robin, Black Country, Ted Sturgeon and The Ears of Johnny Bear
To Rhett Butler and Jiminy Cricket
To Matthew Arnold, Robert Frost and The Demolished Man
To What Mad Universe
To Dante, Dr. Lao and Dick Tracy
To Punch, the Immortal Liar, and The Girls in Their Summer Dresses
To The Man in the Iron Mask
To Marco Polo and The Martian Chronicles
To Bogie and The Maltese Falcon
To Flash Gordon, Prince Valiant, Krazy Kat and The Dance of The Dead
To Thomas Wolfe
To The Unicorn in the Garden
To Hammett and Chandler and You Play the Black and the Red Comes Up
To Papa Hemingway, Mickey Spillane and Popeye the Sailor Man
To Fancies and Goodnights

To a Diamond as Big as the Ritz and a Blood Wedding in Chicago
To Beauty and the Beast
To The Daredevil Dogs of the Air, The Dawn Patrol and The Long, Loud Silence
To Doug Fairbanks, Errol Flynn and The Keystone Kops
To Tarzan and The Land That Time Forgot
To Tom Swift, Huck Finn and Oliver Twist
To Citizen Kane, Sinbad and They Shoot Horses, Don't They?
To Ali Baba, The Marx Brothers and Dangerous Dan McGrew
To The Beanstalk
To The Lone Ranger, Little Orphan Annie and The Space Merchants
To The Day The Earth Stood Still
To The Highwayman
To Kazan, The Time Machine and Don't Cry for Me
To Captain Midnight and Lights Out
To Shackleton, Terry and the Pirates, Richard the Lionheart and The Rats in the Walls
To The Most Dangerous Game
To Lil' Abner, S. J. Perelman and Smoky Stover
To The Seven Dwarfs and Mandrake the Magician
To Billy the Kid, Geronimo, Stephen Vincent Benét and The House of Usher
To The Hound of the Baskervilles and The Ship of Ishtar
To Robin Hood, Scarface and Tommy Udo
To Frederick Schiller Faust who was Max Brand who was Evan Evans who was George Challis who was . . .
To Astounding, Amazing, Fantastic, Startling, Unknown, Galaxy, Weird Tales, Planet Stories, Black Mask and The Magazine of Fantasy and Science Fiction
To Rhysling, Blind Singer of the Spaceways

AND, WITH LOVE

To The Green Hills of Earth

The seeds of the Little War were planted in a
restless summer during the mid-1960s,
with sit-ins and student demonstrations as youth
tested its strength.

By the early 1970s over 75 per cent of the people
living on earth
were under twenty-one years of age.

The population continued to climb—and
with it the youth percentage.

In the 1980s the figure was 79.7 per cent.

In the 1990s, 82.4 per cent.

In the year 2000—critical mass.

10

Her hair was matted, her face streaked and swollen. One knee oozed slow blood; she'd cut it on a steel abutment. A stitching pain lived in her side.

She ran.

There was a high lovers' moon and the night was full of shapes. Shadows slid on shadows.

When had she crossed the river? Was it last night or the night before? Where was she now? She didn't know.

Off to her right she could see an unending length of metalmesh beyond a stretch of dead asphalt. Far out on the pavement sea was a cluster of teeter-swings. An industrial nursery; it had to be Stoneham or Sunrise.

Perhaps her baby was there!

She veered to the left, away from the mesh, into the deep nightblack between buildings. Abruptly she found her passage blocked by a high board barrier. She turned. Maybe she could double back over the river.

If she could only rest.

Wait! She froze, remained motionless. There was someone in the shadows ahead. A silent scream ripped at her throat.

Sandman!

Panic drove her heart against her chest in shuddering strokes. She spun about, clawed at the blistered boards, her fingernails breaking as she sought a grip on the coarse wood. The fence was too high.

For an instant (a century?) she hung there, trying to will her muscles to lift her oh-so-heavy body, but all the energy was gone. Something tore inside her, and she crumpled at the base of the wood.

Huddled into herself, she studied the char-black flower crystal centered in the palm of her right hand. A few days ago it had been a warm blood-red – just as seven years before it had been electric-blue, and seven years earlier, sun-yellow. A color for each seven years of her life. Now she was twenty-one and her flower was dull black. Sleep black. Death black.

The figure moved calmly toward her, across the moonpavement. She didn't look up. She stared at her palm, because her future and her past were written there. All of her days and her nights and her fears and her hopes.

Why had she believed in Sanctuary? Insane. Impossible. Why hadn't she been like all the others who had accepted Sleep?

Now the dark figure, in black, stood over her, but she did not look up. She didn't beg because begging was useless.

Instead she remade the world.

She was not here, outlawed and condemned, shamed and terrified; she was in Sanctuary – on a wide, wind-lazy meadow beside a cool stream of silver – a world in which time did not exist.

Then why was her hand scrabbling under her torn clothing for the vibroknife she'd hidden there? Why the urgency to plunge the buzzing steel through breast and rib into her heart? Why?

She saw the Gun come up.

The homer!

She saw the moonlight dazzle off the dark-blue barrel.

The homer!

She saw the pale, tight-set face of the Sandman, and saw his eyes above the Gun, as his fingers whitened on the trigger.

The homer!

There was a soft explosion.

That was the last thing she heard.

And the last thing she felt was raw, blinding agony as the homer struck, ripped and unraveled her.

LOGAN WAS TIRED, but the little man kept talking.

'You know how it is, citizen,' he said. 'Nobody feels like he's done it *all*. All the traveling, all the girls, all the living. I'm no different from anybody else. I'd like to live to be twenty-five, thirty . . . but it just isn't going to happen. And I can accept that. I've got no regrets. None to linger on, I mean. I've lived a good life. I've had my share and nobody can say that Sawyer is a whiner.'

He was talking compulsively. As long as he talked he didn't have to think. Logan had seen a lot of them on Lastday, talking away the final hours.

'You know what I'm going to do?' asked the man, whose palm-flower was blinking red, then black, then red. He didn't wait for a reply. He went on in a rapid voice, telling Logan exactly what he was going to do.

Logan had changed to grays back in DS Headquarters, and he wondered if the man would be talking to him if he were in his black tunic. No doubt he would. Sawyer was obviously the type who went through life unworried about Deep Sleep men and Guns. Which was proper. He was a good citizen, and good citizens made a stable world.

' – and then I'm going over to the Castlemont Glasshouse and get myself three of the youngest, prettiest girls in the stag-room. One will be blonde. You know, with deep-blue eyes and blue-white hair. Then I'll get one with short black hair and one with golden-brown skin. Three beauties. I hear they'll do anything for you when you're on Lastday.'

The man looked at his palm. The flower bloomed red, then black, then red. 'Did you ever wonder if the Thinker makes mistakes, the same as people do? Because it doesn't seem like I've turned twenty-one. It really doesn't. It seems I turned fourteen maybe five years ago. That would make me just nineteen.' He said this without conviction. 'I remember the day, when my flower changed and I was fourteen. I was in Japan, and it was the first time I'd visited Fujiyama. Wonderful mountain! Inspiring! Ever see it?'

Logan nodded. He'd seen it.

'I sure remember the day. Couldn't have been more than

five years ago – maybe six. Do you think the machine could make that kind of mistake?'

Logan didn't want to remember how many years had passed since *he'd* been fourteen. Of late he had tried not to think about this. His flower was still a steady red, but . . .

'No,' said Sawyer, answering his own question. 'The machine wouldn't make that kind of a mistake.' He was silent for a long moment; then, in a quiet voice, he said, 'I suppose I'm scared.' His flower blinked red, black, red, black.

'Most people are,' said Logan.

'But not *this* scared,' said the man. He swallowed, raised a hand. 'Don't get me wrong, citizen. I'm no coward. I'm not going to run. I have my pride. The system is right, I know that. World can only support so much life. Got to be a way to keep the population down. . . . . I've been loyal and I won't change now.'

The two sat quietly as the rumbling belt carried them up through the threemile complex.

At last the man spoke again: 'Do you really believe that a homer is – is as *terrible* as they say it is?'

'Yes,' said Logan. 'I believe it.'

'What gets me is the way it *finds* a runner. Once it's fired at him, I mean. The way it homes in on the body heat. They say it burns out your whole nervous system. Every nerve in your body.

Logan didn't answer.

The little man's face was gray. A muscle leaped in his cheek. He swallowed. 'God,' he said.

Sawyer drew in a deep breath. A spot of color returned to his face. 'Of course it's necessary. Without the DS men and homers there'd be a lot more runners. We couldn't have that. Runner deserves what he gets, if you ask me. I mean, he doesn't have to run. A Sleepshop isn't so bad, is it? We toured one when I was twelve, me and a friend of mine. In Paris. Clean and nice. It isn't so bad.'

Logan thought of the Sleepshops with their gaily painted interiors, the attendants in soft pastel robes, the electronically augmented angel choirs, the skin spray of Hallucinogen, which wiped away a confused look of suffering and replaced it with a fixed and joyful smile. He thought of the quiet, dim-lit grave room lined with aluminium shelving, and of the neat rows of steelfoil canisters marked with the names and numbers of men.

'No,' said Logan. 'It isn't so bad.'

Sawyer was talking again. 'Sometimes, though, I wonder about those DS men. I could never do it, what they have to do. Not that I'm defending runners. Not scum. I don't defend scum. But I just wonder how a man can fire a homer into – '

'I get off here,' said Logan.

He left the belt.

Logan was annoyed at his action. He didn't live in this part of the complex. His unit was almost a mile beyond, but the man's constant chatter had frayed his patience. He knew this section, of course. A year ago he'd hunted a man here. Runner named Nathan. He closed off the memory.

Idly he began walking the covered thoroughfare.

Ahead was the Jewel Building. Logan paused to survey the vast mural which gave the structure its name – a climbing mosaic composed of tiny bits of fireglass brilliantly arranged to commemorate the Burning of Washington. Orange, purple and raw red flames jeweled halfway up the façade; bodies flamed; buildings smoked and tumbled. Yet the awesome masterwork was flawed, incomplete. Stark, gaping areas broke the pattern. Only the famed muralist Roebler 7 could handle the corrosive fireglass, and when he had accepted Sleep his secret died with him. The project would never be finished.

Directly beneath the mural, a man with a sign. Logan registered shock. The man was about fifteen and rounded, girlish features and large, soulful eyes. A silver fringe of beard silked his chin, and his hair was worn shoulder-length. The sign around his neck said: *RUN!*

He sat, image-still, in the middle of the walkway. Several angry citizens circled him. One of them spat on the bearded man.

'Filth!'

'Scum!'

'Coward!'

The man smiled patiently at his tormentors. He handed each of them a thin scripsheet from a stack in his lap.

'This is disgusting,' said a fat woman, balling the scrip in her hand. 'Unlawful.'

As Logan approached, the man held out one of the sheets. He accepted it.

REJECT SLEEP! RUN!

IF THERE ARE ENOUGH RUNNERS
THERE WON'T BE ENOUGH HOMERS.
THERE WON'T BE ENOUGH DS MEN.
IT IS WRITTEN THAT THE LIFE
SPAN OF MAN IS THREE SCORE
YEARS AND TEN. SEVENTY YEARS!
DON'T SETTLE FOR TWENTY-ONE.
RUN! REJECT SLEEP!

A police paravane settled soundlessly at the edge of the walkway. Logan watched the two lemon-tunicked officers dismount and advance on the bearded man. He did not try to run. They led him away.

The paravane lifted back into the evening sky.

A woman next to Logan clucked her tongue. 'That's the third maniac they've arrested this month. You'd think they were organized. It's frightening.'

A girl in green mistsilks eased out of a doorway and fell into step beside Logan. He ignored her. The darkness had deepened and the sky was splashed with emerging stars. An air-freshener hummed.

Logan stopped to watch the Tri-Dim Report.

The proscenium of the TD Newsbuilding brightened. A familiar 300-foot figure took solid form; he smiled warmly down at the crowd. The tri-dimensional newsman was dressed in Lifeleather trimfits. His giant eyes were clear and guileless.

'Evening, Citizens,' he boomed. 'This is Madison 24 with the latest news. Trouble in the maze tonight. A gypsy gang war on an express platform near Stafford Heights resulted in two deaths. Fourteen individuals were injured, including three gypsies. Police are investigating and there *will* be arrests.' The immense figure paused for dramatic effect, then continued. 'The triple slayer, Harry 7, was apprehended earlier today in the Trancas complex. His friends were invited to see him off in the Hellcar. But not *one* person showed up. Not one.' The giant face nodded sternly. 'Does that tell you something, citizens? It tells me something. Yes, indeed. It tells me that we are a proud, law-loving people, ashamed of runners and killers and that we are – '

Logan stopped listening. He became aware of the girl at his side.

'You're not happy,' the girl in green said. 'I can always tell. I have a gift for knowing, for sensing unhappiness.' Her eyes shone with a fierce intensity. 'I sympathize with unhappy men.'

She placed a soft hand on his waist and pressed lightly. He shook off the hand.

Logan walked away, lengthening his stride.

'I could make you happy,' called the girl. Her voice drifted after him faintly: ' – make you happy.'

Happy. Logan turned the word over in his mind. Restlessness gnawed at him. *You can't buy happiness.* But of course, you could.

The hallucimill on Roeburt was one of the city's largest. The drugs, administered by trained professionals, were non-addictive. Logan had tried several and found that LF produced the happiest effects – Lysergic Foam, an extension of the old LSD formula developed more than a century and a half ago. It required sixty seconds to run a man's bloodstream. After that: expanded consciousness. Synthetic bliss.

'LF,' Logan told the man in white.

'Dosage?'

'Standard.'

'Follow me, please.'

Logan was taken to the blueroom: a small, padded chamber

with a table, a chair and a blue floor. And nothing else.

A woman was coming out of the room. Her face was papery, her eyes still partially glazed.

Logan took the drugflask handed him, swallowed the contents. 'Have a good lift,' the man in white said as he closed the door.

Logan sat down in the chair, keeping his eyes closed for a full minute, allowing the LF to work itself into his blood. Then he relaxed, opened his eyes.

A terrible illumination fired the room, and Logan knew it was going to be a bad lift.

Window, he thought, got to reach the window. It was open when he reached it and he fell out of the window, dropping down rapidly into the heart of the threemile complex.

A short, squat man caught him.

'You were running,' the man said. 'That's fine.'

'No, I was falling. There's a big difference.' It was important that he be understood. 'I fell from a window. *Fell.*'

Logan twisted away, began to run.

He ran through hissing firegalleries. The world smelled of dream dust, and a million voices were dirging the coda to 'Black Flower.'

The short, squat man dropped him with a blow.

'Again,' said the man, crouched.

But Logan had the Gun. He didn't need to take any more of this damned punishment!

He pulled the trigger.

And the world exploded.

On the way out the attendant grinned at Logan. 'You were really lifted. Like another?'

'No, thanks,' said Logan, and left the building.

He didn't feel any better.

On the upper level he slowed. A group of youngsters approached him, their palms glowing like blue fireflies in the soft dark. As they passed, Logan heard snatches of heated argument.

'The Reddies don't remember *we've* got rights, too.'

'They just better begin to – '

Echoes of the Little War.

Logan moved on, toward the play of colored lights on the glasshouse ahead.

The big dome was frosted in white, and interior images were indistinct. A contortion of naked, massed bodies formed a high, arched entrance, and the steps leading inside were illumined from below.

PLEASURE gleamed a step.

SATISFACTION gleamed another.

RARE DELIGHTS gleamed a third.

Logan entered.

'Your pleasure is our pleasure, sir,' a flax-haired girl said to him mechanically. She was seated at a flow desk and wore red satin transpants.

Logan placed his right palm flat to the desk. An inaudible click: the desk would bill him later for the visit.

He walked into the stageroom.

It was awash in sexuality. Here were beach girls from Mexico and California, Japanese maidens with shy eyes, Italian girls with mooned bodies, pert Irish lads, slim exotics from Calcutta, cool Englishwomen and full-figured French girls. All here because they were lonely or bored or oversexed; because they were looking for someone new or escaping from someone old – or for no reason at all except that the glasshouse was here to be used and it was a time for mingling and touching in a shadow-search for love. *You never find the people that you go to meet in dreams. . . .*

A girl with a blue palm swayed toward Logan; she was Eurasian and, at thirteen, a year away from womanhood. 'I'm adept,' she said. 'You'll find me skilled beyond any others.'

Logan ignored her, gesturing to an older girl with red hair flowing along her back. She was swan-white with deep-lashed eyes of coral. 'You,' he said.

The girl glided in his direction, the thin silk of her gown clouding behind her. 'Not me,' she laughed, linking arms with a blue-gold blonde.

Logan was irritated. Ordinarily he would have been excited, flushed with anticipation. Tonight he felt dulled by what he saw.

He waved another female to him, a lithe girl with Slavic features and full hips. She smiled, took his hand.

They caught a riser up, passing tier on tier, stepped into a glass hall, moved in darkness to a glass room.

The girl told him that her name was Karenya 3.

'I'm a three also,' Logan told her.

'Don't talk,' she said feverishly. 'Why do men always want to talk?'

Logan sat down on the bed and began to unbutton his shirt. The girl was already nude, having cast aside a thin garment of spun gauze.

How many times have I come to a place like this? he asked himself. To a lonely, empty house of glass. . . .

Glass all around them. Glass walls and ceilings and floors. The bed, glass fiber. The chairs and tables, glass. The building was one vast transparent globe, shot periodically with colored lights.

Each room was equipped to illumine itself at irregular intervals, but it was impossible to determine just *when* a room would flare into brightness. Caught in the act of lovemaking, a couple would suddenly find themselves tangled in a wash of silver, or gold, or red, yellow or green. Other couples, around, above and below, would be able to watch them from glass floors, walls, ceilings. Then the light would die – to spring on in another chamber.

'Here,' said the girl. 'Lie here.'

Logan eased into the glassfoam bedding. She guided his hand, and he gave himself over to this woman, holding and stroking her body in the darkness.

'Look!' she cried.

In the tier above them, bathed in hot gold, a man and a woman writhed in a love heat. Then darkness.

The night deepened.

Logan and Karenya were frozen in silver, arms and legs twined. They were conscious of the eyes around them in the dome, watching hungrily.

Darkness again.

Light bloomed, died, flared and died in the love depths of the structure.

Until dawn sketched the glasshouse.

The loving was over and done.

'Please visit us again,' said the flax-haired girl in transpants.

Logan exited, saying nothing.

Time for duty. No time to sleep. Logan went home to his unit, took a Detoxic, flushing his system, but this didn't seem to help. His eyes felt grainy; his muscles ached. He suited up and went down to headquarters.

Francis was there when he walked in.

The tall man grinned at him. 'You look ripped,' he said. 'Bad night?'

Francis never looked ripped. No lifts or glasshouses for him. Not before a job anyway. Francis was cool and clearheaded and sure of himself. Why couldn't *he* be like that?

Actually there were few DS men who possessed the skill and drive of this friendless, loveless man with the mantis-thin body and the black eyes of a hunting cat. Precise, deadly, ruthless. Only the Thinker knew how many runners Francis had Gunned.

And what does he think of me? Logan asked himself. Always the casual grin, the light remark, telling you nothing. But judging every move.

The hallway was wide and gray and cold, yet Logan felt the warm sweat gathering under his tunic and along his hands as he walked.

He'd be all right once he had the Gun. He'd be fine; he always was. Soon he'd be hunting, man-tracking a runner somewhere in the city, doing his job as he had done it for years.

He'd be all right then.

The hallway ended. The two men faced a smooth section of wallmetal.

'Identities,' said a metallic voice.

Each man pressed the palm of his right hand against the wall.

A panel slid back, revealing an alcove lined with worn black velvet. Gleaming in the velvet, long-barreled and waiting, were the Guns.

Only a DS man could carry a Gun. Each weapon was coded to the operative's hand pattern, set to detonate on any other human contact.

Logan reached in and closed his fingers around the big pearl-handled revolver, drawing it free of its snug velvet nest. He checked it; full load, six charges: tangler, ripper, needler, nitro, vapor – and homer.

Already the sense of power was building in him as he held the Gun, weighing it in his hand, letting the light slide along the chased-silver barrel. Weapons shaped like these had kept the peace in towns named Abilene and Dodge and Fargo. Called 'sixguns' then, their chambers held lead bullets. Now, centuries later, their cargo was far deadlier.

'Identities,' demanded the wall again.

The two men ignored the malfunction.

'Identities, please.'

The report room hummed.

The room clicked and flashed, metallically coding, decoding, indexing, weighing, processing, filing, tracking – rendering its impersonal machine data to the DS operatives who moved before its faceted wall of insect lights.

A dispatcher looked up, saw them. His face was dry and chafed, his expression harried. He picked out a scan record and bustled toward them.

'We've been jammed here,' he said irritably. 'Stanhope's in the field and I can't locate Webster 16. We've got a runner in Pavilion, moving east.'

The room was a cross-mixture of voices.

'Come in Kelly 4. DS at Morningside seven twelve.'

'Come in Stanhope. Your man is in the maze.'

'Evans 9. Confirm. Runner's destination recorded seven-o-four as Phoenix. Mazecar waiting at Palisades. Confirm.'

Logan swept the alert board. A light went on at the third level, east sector.

'Who takes him?' he asked.

'You do,' said the dispatcher. 'Francis is on backup.'

'All right,' said Logan. 'Give me a scan.'

'Name: Doyle 10-14302. His flower blacked at five thirty-nine. That would be' – he checked a wallchron – 'eighteen minutes ago. He's heading east, up through the complex. So far he's avoided the maze. I make it he knows about the platform scanners. He's going for Arcade. Cagy. He must know the firegalleries interfere with a DS scope. The rest is on the board. Good hunting.'

Logan began to plot the alarm trail as it came in over the circuits. A light went on at fourth level east. Citizen alarm. Logan noted it. Ordinary citizens are your best allies when a runner is loose. Another light at level five. Logan waited for the third light before he left the alert room.

In Central Files he punched Doyle 10–14302. The slot instantly produced the physical file on the runner: a TD photo, vital statistics, pore patterns, names of known friends and associates.

Logan checked Doyle's flower history: *YELLOW:* Childhood. Birth to seven years: machine-reared in a Missouri nursery. No unusual traits noted. *BLUE:* Boyhood. Seven to fourteen. The usual pattern. Lived in a dozen states, roamed Europe. No arrests. *RED:* Manhood. Fourteen to twenty-one. Rebel. Arrested at sixteen for blocking a DS man on a hunt. Pairups with three women, one of whom suspected of aiding runners. Has a twin sister, Jessica 6, whose record is clear.

Logan studied Doyle's photo.

The runner was a big man, his own size, dark hair, strong memorable face with a wide jaw, straight nose. Slight scar above the right eye. Logan would know Doyle when he found him.

He unclipped the small black Follower scope from his belt and tuned in to Doyle's flower pattern. Then he returned to the alert room.

A new light on the board: the upper concourse of the complex.

Francis was at Logan's elbow. 'This is no ordinary runner,' he said. 'I've been tracking him on the board. He's got a destination – and he's not making any mistakes. Call me if you need me. That's what backup's for.'

Logan nodded tightly. He snugged his Gun into its tunic holster, checked the scope on his Follower and left the room.

The hunt began.

Logan got off the belt at the main concourse as his quarry emerged from a public riser. Doyle saw the black tunic and dipped into a crowd. Logan stuck with him as the crowd thinned. He was still heading east – toward Arcade.

He'd be hard to track in the vast pleasure center. Logan moved to head him off, but the runner reversed direction and caught a slide. Good. The man was moving downward again. Let him run.

Logan watched Doyle's progress on the Follower, represented by a tiny alarm trail of flashing light dots.

Time to give him another nudge.

At Morningside Heights and Pavilion he picked up Doyle again. The man *must* know about the maze scanners, Logan thought; the dispatcher was correct in this. Doyle had passed up a dozen chances to go underground. He was swinging east again, making another bid for Arcade.

Logan showed himself in the crowd-surge. There's nothing to equal the flash of a black tunic to instill panic in a runner. And panic would kill him. Panic and a homer. Logan moved up a level, to place himself between the runner and Arcade.

Doyle didn't panic.

He was smart. This was no frightened psychotic who'd come unhinged the moment his hand blacked. He'd dodged and shifted like a chess player, calculating each move. He stayed in crowds; he didn't let himself get locked in on a single level, but stayed close to the main lifts which offered him mobility.

Logan felt a reluctant admiration for this man. Doyle could

have made a fine DS operative. He had the instincts and grace of a hunter. He seemed aware of DS limitations and exploited the knowledge.

Enough of this, Logan warned himself. Let's get on with the job. Fill up with coldness and hate. Build the image of a jackal, a warped coward running from justice. Weak, spineless, selfish. Living beyond his time.

Chase, capture and *kill*.

Logan watched the Follower as one of the tiny light dots neared his position. Doyle should come out of the lift – now.

The man stepped into view.

Logan brought up the Gun. He caught a white, shocked face in the sights. It would be an easy shot, a clean kill. In that moment Doyle saw his danger. He tried to back into the lift.

Logan had him. Before Doyle could take cover the heat-sensing element in the homer would seek him out and destroy him. Logan's finger curled on the trigger. He hesitated.

The brief hesitation cost him the shot. Doyle was in the lift, headed down.

Logan swore tensely. What had gone wrong? Why hadn't he Gunned the man?

On the scope he watched the dot descend two levels and head south. Once again Logan moved to cut the runner off. He dropped three levels, circled to the foot of the slope ramp, waiting. This time he would not miss.

When Doyle appeared he was holding a human shield. A girl, ten or eleven. Struggling in Doyle's arms, she reacted in terror as she saw the DS man.

Logan flipped the chamber to tangler and fired the charge. Doyle flung the girl forward into it. The blast of silver threads enveloped her, clouding over her upper body in a tight webbing. Already Doyle was running again.

A paravane was cruising the area and Logan alerted it. The police would bring the delicate equipment needed to soften and dissolve the threads without harming the girl. Logan put her out of his mind.

The dot was ahead.

The main thoroughfare was thick with citizens. Among

them, moving away, was Doyle. No good trying to fire a homer in this press of bodies. Too dangerous. There was always the chance that an onlooker would step in front of the charge and divert its course. To a homer, seeking a normal 98.6° in body temperature, one man was like another. Logan would have to be certain of his shot. The only sure way to take out a runner in a packed crowd was to walk directly up to him, jam the Gun in his stomach and fire. But Doyle was too fast to allow this.

The hunt continued.

Doyle was veering east again. Making another try for Arcade. Logan moved quickly to intercept him, riding an express belt to the east edge of the concourse. This should do it; Doyle would walk right into his Gun.

But he didn't. Something was wrong. It had been a feint. The dot was going down through the complex – heading *west*. Toward Cathedral.

Bad. In Cathedral he could lose Doyle forever, and that isn't going to happen.

Logan put in a call to backup.

'He tricked me, and I went for it,' he told Francis. 'It's up to you to cut him off at the stone bridge into Cathedral. I'll meet you there.'

Francis didn't waste time with a reply.

He clicked off.

Cathedral: a festering sore in the side of Greater Los Angeles, an area of rubble and dust and burned-out buildings, a place of shadow and pollution, of stealth and sudden death. Cubscout territory. If Doyle cleared the bridge the cubs would take him. The kill would be theirs – and that was bad for the record.

Logan was well aware of Cathedral's blood history. Of the runners who never came out. Of the muggings. Of the unchecked violence. Even the police avoided Cathedral. With good reason. They'd sent in a cleanup squad the previous summer to tame the cubs. Logan had known some of the men in that squad: Sanson and Bradley and Wilson 9, all good officers. They'd walked into the jaws of the crocodile and the jaws had closed. None of the squad survived.

You didn't take chances in Cathedral.

The express belt broke down at River Level, and Logan was forced to take a walkway to Sutton and use the out ramp. These transit breaks had been occurring more and more frequently of late. And since the Thinker was self-repairing, or *supposed* to be, there was nothing anyone could do about the situation.

When Logan reached the east side of the long stone bridge which fed into Cathedral he found Francis slumped against the spillwall.

'Chopped me from behind,' he said, rubbing his head. 'Your runner's tough.'

Logan scanned the area. The scope indicated that Doyle was very near. A shadow on the bridge. Logan raised his Gun for a shot, but couldn't get a clear view of the man.

Doyle kept under the stone parapet, scuttling crablike across the span, keeping the thick masonry between himself and the Gun.

'He's over,' said Francis.

The runner had cleared the end of the bridge and ducked behind the tumbled ruins of a warehouse. But within seconds he reappeared, retreating from a tide of moving colors, quick shapes.

'Cubs!' breathed Logan.

He studied the cubscouts. There was something odd and fragmented about their movements as they converged on Doyle. Then he realised what he was seeing. He heard Francis swear softly. 'They're on Muscle.'

The small figures moved in a continual blur of motion, darting and flitting like earthbound dragonflies.

Where do they get the stuff? Logan wondered. Muscle had been outlawed since the Little War. Originally developed for armed combat, the drug was designed to speed up reactions. It increased a man's strength tenfold, giving him ample time to deal with an enemy. But its action was too violent to control; it forced the heart to do a day's work in minutes. A man lived impossibly fast with Muscle in the bloodstream. Only the very young could use it.

Logan felt the flesh on his scalp tighten as he watched the incredibly swift boy-shapes attack the runner. Under Muscle a stick in a fist becomes a steel hammer – and the swarming cubs were cutting Doyle to pieces. He was on the ground, hands outstretched to ward off the cubs, but they were killing him. They were all around him in a rippling, weaving circle; and each wet, bone-shattering blow brought Doyle closer to death.

Logan and Francis were crouched behind a wall of rubble facing the action in the clearing ahead of them.

'We'll try vapor,' said Francis. 'Plug up.'

They inserted nose filters. Francis flipped the Gun to V, braced the weapon against the top of the wall, fired.

The gas charge took immediate effect, driving the cubs back in a broken wave.

Doyle lay huddled and unmoving in the center of the clearing.

'Let's check him,' said Logan.

'I can handle it. You cover me.'

Before Francis could reach the runner the cubs regrouped to cut him off. They backed the DS man into a shallow pocket of stone to one side of the open ground. A second wave came for Logan.

He fired a nitro into the group, and three of the cubs were torn about by the blast. This stopped them long enough for Logan to reach Doyle.

The man's face was a mosaic of blood and bone-ends; his mouth moved convulsively. A word. The runner was repeating a word.

Logan leaned closer to catch the broken whisper: 'Sanctuary.'

Logan tensed. The runner's head fell back loosely; his fingers uncurled. A small glittering object fell from his left hand. A punchkey. Logan pocketed it.

The flat, dry crack of a ripper. Francis was effectively dealing with his attackers. He came into the clearing and stepped quickly to Doyle.

'Alive?' he asked.

'Dead,' said Logan.

Francis stared sourly down at the unbreathing man, obviously disappointed, cheated of a prize. Then slowly he raised his Gun and fired a blister charge into the body.

The dead runner flamed and danced into sudden ash.

'Let's go,' said Francis.

On the way back to headquarters, riding beside Francis in the shuttle, Logan kept his right fist closed against his side. He didn't want to see the flower in his palm.

It was blinking.

9

He cat-prowls the corridors.

He stops in front of the Gunwall. Logan's Gun is still not there.

He paces, waits.

He hears a guarded whisper not meant for his ears: 'Old Francis is on to something,' says a voice.

'They say the cubs cheated him out of a runner.'

'That isn't it. He's on to something.'

He doesn't react to this.

He shadow-glides the gray halls.

He is a violence, contained.

He moves back to the Gunwall, stares, moves away.

He checks the time: 7:30.

Fact: Logan has not returned with his Gun.

Fact: Logan is on Lastday.

He instructs the techs to rig a Gun trace, tuned to Logan's weapon. When the Gun is fired it will register its location on the board.

He sits, face illuminated by ghost lights from the glowing circuits.

He waits.

EVENING . . .

WHEN LOGAN WALKED into his living unit young Abe Lincoln was there, splitting logs in the center of the room. Logan automatically punched a wall stud and the president was sucked, hissing, back into the Tri-Dim.

He stripped, bathed, changed to grays and dialed a meal and a Scotch. Sipping the iced drink, Logan stared at his palm, at the blinking crystal flower.

Lastday. Twenty-four hours in which to live. Then his flower would go black and it would be time to turn himself in for Sleep.

Twenty-four hours.

Logan picked up the silver punchkey from the bed.

Runners say *please*; runners say *help*; runners say *mercy*; runners say *don't*.

Doyle had said *Sanctuary*.

And Logan held a key which might lead to it, to a goal never proved to exist, to a place which *could* not exist. Not in this world. Not for a runner in 2116.

But what if Sanctuary were a reality? A place where runners were safe from the Gun. What if he, Logan 3, could find it and destroy it in the last twenty-four hours of his life? His existence would be justified; he'd be a world hero; his life would end in glory.

It would be a risk worth taking. And the key to the quest lay in his hand.

Do it.

Logan walked to the communideck. The silver key slid easily into the slot. Inside the flat housing, tiny indentations in the stamped metal made electrical connections. The wallscreen lightened.

A girl in vented peekaboos regarded Logan. She was perhaps sixteen, with dead, flat eyes. Her body was slim-breasted and angular. 'Call back later,' she said. 'I'm going out.'

'I'm calling *now*,' said Logan.

'Have you got a name?'

'I've got a name.' He let it rest at that.

A spark of interest in the flat eyes. 'But you're keeping it to yourself.'

'There's no sanctuary in passing out random identities,' said Logan, leaning slightly on the word sanctuary.

Her gaze did not flicker.

This didn't feel right. Not right at all. The runner could have been babbling. Maybe he was acting on a false lead.

'Who gave you my key?' the girl asked.

'A friend.'

'I'm going out.'

'You said that.'

'To a party. I'm expected.'

'I could meet you there,' said Logan.

She studied him speculatively.

'Halstead complex. West wing. Fourth level. Living unit 2582. Got that?'

Logan nodded.

'I really shouldn't be inviting strangers,' she said. 'If you're . . . not up to the party I'll be to blame.'

'I'm up to it,' said Logan, 'and anything else.' He kept his face impassive.

'We'll see.'

She said one last thing before she blacked. 'I'm Lilith 4. I think you'll find me . . . helpful.'

The screen died.

Logan let out a breath. It sounded like a word. The word it sounded like was 'Sanctuary.'

The party in unit 2582 was getting into full stride when Logan arrived. The door was opened by a mouse-faced man in orange trims. He was quite intoxicated.

'The tree of cruelty often blooms in the fertile soil of love,' he said.

'I'm sure it does,' said Logan, scanning the crowded room for Lilith.

'The boy seeks, the man finds. That's a poem. I write them, you know.'

'I didn't know,' said Logan. The girl was not in the crowd. Perhaps she'd been delayed or had changed her mind about meeting him.

'One of my poems was read on TD. Called "Womb Wood." Like to hear it?'

Logan said nothing.

'In the woods of the womb,
She walked.
In a whirl of red wounds,
She fell.
Heart bursting like a plum
In the bracelets of her breasts.'

Logan sat down on a flowcouch built into the wall. The poet continued to talk, obviously determined to elicit praise.

'That poem received a great deal of very favorable comment. I'm quite famous, you know.'

'Fine,' said Logan.

A toad of a man scuttled up with a foaming mug in his hand. 'Try this,' he said. Logan caught the slightly sour odor of fermentation. 'It's Volney's home brew. We've got a whole keg of it. It's nothing like the beer from the slots. He's a real artist, Volney is. Puts musk raisins in it.'

'I prefer Scotch.'

'That's your loss, citizen.'

Logan dialed a Scotch. It was taken from him by a red-haired girl in slashvelvets. She downed it hurriedly.

'Wonderful!' she said. Her green eyes were alcohol flushed. She offered Logan a cigarette.

'No, thanks.'

'Don't be afraid to,' she urged him. 'There's a police payoff in this area. No tobacco raids. Go ahead.'

'No, thanks.'

The girl took offense. 'Afraid to smoke, aren't you? You men! Cowards. Every one of you cowards. I was on pairup with a merchantman until last week. Then we broke it. Know why?'

'Why?' asked Logan.

'Because. Because he lacked the essentials. He was content. Content to *be* content. He had his business and he had me and that's all he wanted. I need a man who wants what he doesn't have. That make sense to you, citizen?'

'Maybe you don't need a man. Maybe you need a boy.'

'I tried a boy. Eleven. He was good for a while, but I got so I hated his young face. I'm fifteen – and a woman needs a man. How old are you?'

'Old enough,' said Logan, keeping his right hand closed. The flower blinked warmly in palmflesh. He could feel its heat against his fingertips.

'How about a pairup?'

'No. No, thanks.'

The green eyes chilled. 'Is that all you can say – "no, thanks"?' The girl stood up, weaved away.

Logan sighed. *Where* was Lilith?

The door slid open and a fat-bellied man eased in, bearing a double armload of clothing and accessories. His voice shrilled in falsetto. 'Hail, fellow lungblasters and glassmasters and livefasters! Hail, fellow peepers! The gear is here.' The fatman pasted a talk puppet grin on his face and began strutting the room in high-pumping steps. 'Gear up! Everybody gear up!'

'Been waiting long?' Lilith 4 grinned down at Logan; a pink cigarette dangled smoke from her glitter-coated lips. She was bare-hipped in silver snakeskins.

'Let's talk,' said Logan. 'You know why I'm here.'

The fatman bustled importantly up to them. He thrust a black knit bodystocking and crepe stretchsoles at them. 'Gear up, you two,' he said, clapping his meaty hands. 'Let's peep!'

'We'll be partners,' declared Lilith. 'You said you were up to it.'

Logan took the clothing, moved to a changeroom and slipped out of his grays. He'd have to stow the Gun somewhere; no place to conceal it in the skintight bodysuit. At least he'd left the spare ammo packs in his unit; figuring that the six charges in the weapon should see him through. Now he was grateful for this decision. Less bulk to worry about. He slipped the Gun into an alcove, gambling that no one would have occasion to search the closet.

'You have Greek shoulders,' said the mouse-faced poet,

who was beginning to gear up next to him.

Logan grunted and returned to Lilith, who was already dressed and ready. She offered him a Scotch.

'Thanks, I can *use* this!' He tipped the glass to his lips.

A dozen dark-garbed men and women waited in the central chamber. They joined them, and the girl handed Logan a pair of smokegoggles. 'Wear these on the ledge.'

Six black-light cameras were arranged neatly on a table. One camera per couple.

'Righty, righty,' said the fatman, signaling for attention. 'Now all you peepers know what to do?'

'Stop being a damn woman, Sharps,' said a bored voice, 'and get on with it.'

Sharps glanced petulantly at the speaker. '*I'm* in charge. The cameras belong to me!'

'And it's *your* alcohol and *your* tobacco and *your* living unit. For which we are all duly grateful. So let's peep.'

Sharps made an obscene gesture. He waved the first couple off. In pairs, the players left the chamber through a ceiling-high view window.

Logan found himself kneeling beside Lilith on a narrow ledge high in the complex. Below them, the great city was alive with snakes of light. He saw the rows of blinking glasshouses near Hurley Square and, beyond, the dazzle of Arcade. The fire galleries sent up their rose glow, staining the edge of the night sky.

It was a long way down.

He shifted the camera and gripped the alum-ribbing of the building wall. Wind slicked between the box beams, threatening to pull him from the ledge.

Lilith crawled into the liquid dark, edging in front of Logan. Keeping his eye on the feminine sway of her dark bottom, he followed.

When the girl stopped he said, 'Talk. We're alone now.' He couldn't see her face behind the goggles.

'First we peep,' she said. '*Then* we talk.'

'Why not now?'

'If we return to the party without film they'll suspect something. Sharps is not the fool he seems. They'll ask questions we might not want to answer.'

High in the complex, a full half-mile above them, a police paravane ran its pinlight along the ledges.

'Keep in shadow,' said Lilith. 'They patrol these landings. We have to be careful.'

Logan knew the game was illegal, and he didn't want the police stopping him. If he got picked up without the Gun he would not be able to prove his identity. They'd have to check him out. If he *had* the Gun, and revealed himself, the girl would close the door on Sanctuary. Either way, he couldn't afford to be stopped.

He'd be careful.

With a cat's litheness, the girl swung, hand over hand, along a guy wire leading to the next ledge. Logan slung the camera over one shoulder and followed.

Most of the windows they could reach were blacked. Other units were unoccupied.

Lilith pointed downward. 'I think something's happening in there,' she said.

The window she'd indicated was closed but not blacked.

The girl took out a slim wire with an earplug at one end and a wallcup on the other. She pressed the cup against the building, the plug in her ear. She smiled.

'Have a listen,' she said, passing the earplug to Logan.

Through the miniature amplifier he could hear voices husky with love. A man and woman. Sighs. The rub of skin on skin.

'Give me the camera,' whispered Lilith. 'And grab my ankles. I'm going down for a shot.'

Logan braced himself. He clung to the girl's legs as she slipped off the ledge, head first. Lilith dangled in space just in front of the dark window. Below her: a mile-deep emptiness, a stagger of steel and glass and box beam units.

Logan leaned back, feet gripping the stone, feeling his leg muscles protest. The camera whirred. 'Up!' the girl whispered.

He pulled her back to the ledge. 'How did you know I could hang on to you?'

'I didn't,' she said. 'That's part of the lift.'

Did she really know anything about Sanctuary? Or was she simply some danger-sick female out for thrills? Logan didn't know. Yet.

A pinlight raked the building. Police!

They melted into shadow. The patrol paravane ghosted past them and continued on its way.

'You're doing fine,' the girl said.

'Can't we talk now?'

She laughed – and crawled off with Logan behind her.

They climbed upward, along ridged metal, their suction stretchsoles aiding the ascent. On the roof Lilith said, 'Jump!'

She leaped into space, cleared a gap between units, and landed in a garden patio. He made the jump, almost losing his balance.

The patio was deserted.

On the adjoining level, however, the girl found fresh prey. 'You take them this time,' she said to Logan.

He aimed the camera, fingered it into whirring motion.

'Good,' said the girl. 'That's prime peeping. Now we – '

'Now we talk – or I pitch you over this ledge. I've had enough of your nonsense.'

'You'd really do it, wouldn't you?' Her voice held excitement.

'I really would.'

'All right . . . what do you know about Sanctuary?'

'I know it's where I want to go.'

'Where did you get my key?' She watched him carefully.

His lips felt loose. He giggled foolishly. 'From . . . from the same place all runners get theirs.'

He giggled again. *What was happening to him?* The hard aluminium ledge rippled, fell away. He was floating out in space with the wind crying around him.

'Answer the question!' the girl's voice whispered intensely at his ear.

Logan found himself singing: 'Angerman was . . . filled with fury, He the judge and he the jury . . .'

Logan babbled happily. He was poised in air, looking down at himself sprawled on the ledge. He watched Lilith cuff him across the mouth. He watched her grab his hair and bend his head back.

'The *key* – where did you get the key?'

'Man named 10, named 10, named 10 . . . named Doyle 10.'

Logan's neck ached.

'Angerman, pursuing faster,' he sang. 'Ang – Angerman, the angry master.'

He stood up rigidly, with the girl clinging to him. The world was no longer dark; it was filled with blazing orange music which stabbed his eyes.

'Did you kill Doyle?'

The orange music stroked him. 'Cubs . . . cubs killed him.'

Logan stepped off the ledge. Instinctively he reached out; his clawing fingers found a grip. His head was clearing as he kicked at air. His right foot lodged on a metal projection and slowly, inch by inch, he drew himself back on to the ledge.

He lay, stomach down, gasping for breath. The girl. She'd drugged his Scotch. With Truthtell. *Had he told her too much?*

'What now?' he asked.

'Go see Doc,' she said sweetly. 'He's your next contact.'

'Doc who?'

'In Arcade. Look for THE NEW YOU. That's his place.'

Logan nodded.

'Now we go back to Sharps and turn in our peeps. Some lift, eh?'

'Sure,' said Logan. 'Some lift.'

He left the belt at the Beverly overpass and began threading his way through Arcade.

The immense pleasure center formed a never-ending human logjam. Arcade had not closed its doors to funseekers for over fifty years. The place was a vast crazy quilt of hallucimills, Re-Live parlors and firegalleries.

Signs screamed and moaned in smoky colors: *RE-LIVE THAT FIRST EMBRACE!* (A gaudy Tri-Dim on a ribbed platform depicting two nude youngsters in a torrid tangle.)

RE-LIVE THOSE PRECIOUS MOMENTS! (A wild-eyed boy riding a flamed devilstick through a mock sky.) *RE-LIVE! RE-LIVE! RE-LIVE!*

Noise gonged; a thousand odors mingled; hawkers cried their wares. Here night was day and day was night.

'Wanta good time, citizen?' A man with one arm and a fog voice beckoned him toward a swinging door.

Logan passed him quickly.

He saw the sign he was looking for. It hit the window in a sulfurous shower and withdrew, hit and withdrew into the darkness behind the black glass. *THE NEW YOU . . . THE NEW YOU . . . THE NEW YOU. . . .*

Logan entered the shop.

The waiting room was the color of ashes. The scattered pieces of furniture were faded, worn. Even the air in the room seemed used. An ancient chrome-plated desk hunched in one corner, and behind it sat a young woman in soiled whites. Her face was pale and predatory. She regarded Logan suspiciously. 'You want Doc?'

'I want Sanctuary.'

The girl wet her lips with a small pink tongue. 'Then you want Doc.'

She rose listlessly, crossed to Logan. 'Hand,' she said. He held up his right hand, palm out. Red-black-red-black-red-black. . . .

'C'mon,' she said. 'Follow through for the new you.'

She led him down a musty hallway and into a large room smelling of metal. Logan recognized the thing in the center of the alum floor; he felt himself ice up. *Table!* The machine loomed over a flat metal bed that was grooved and slotted and equipped with fastening devices.

'There's not another like her outside a hospital between here and New Alaska,' said a harsh, confident voice.

Logan whirled to face a thick-bodied sixteen-year-old. The man's body features were split by a crooked-toothed smile. He wore a long gray smock which extended down to his shoe tops. Doc.

'A little edgy, are you? Well, that's natural. Runners are

scared people. Least you got enough sense to start before your flower blacks. It's tougher then, with the Sandmen on to you. What'll it be, face job or full body? Could add a couple inches to those legs.'

'Just the face,' said Logan.

'Got no time, is that it? Runners never got time.' A note of sad regret in the voice. 'I won't ask your name. I don't want to know it. You got the punchkey and that's good enough for me. Ballard knows who to give them to.'

Ballard! Logan's mind leaped. The world's oldest man. A story to frighten children with. A legend. A subject for folk chants. Was there actually such a man – the force behind Sanctuary?

'Holly will get you ready. If you're worried about the Table, don't be. They call me Doc, but I'm a trained mech. A real mechanic. Give me a basket of transistors and a pound of platinum sponge and I can make anything. You're in good hands, believe what I tell you.'

As he talked, the girl came forward to unbutton the collar of Logan's shirt. The Gun was stuffed into his waistband, and he wondered if they'd want all his clothes off. Hiding the Gun would be impossible here.

'Ask me what I'm doing in a shop like this if I'm so handy. I got my reasons. I make out. A little Muscle for the cubs, a sex lift now and then, a face job for Ballard – maybe a body change for some sick citizen who's tired of himself. Adds up. I do all right.'

The girl was brushing her fingertips lightly down Logan's arms. There was a deep-blue spark in her eyes. 'I'm Holly,' she said softly. 'Holly 13. In ancient times they said my number was unlucky. Do you believe in luck?'

Doc aimed another crooked smile at Logan. 'Holly don't work for the money. She gets her lift out of watching the Table – and *other* things.' His smile became a dry chuckle. 'Back in a minute.'

'Do I need to undress?' Logan asked the girl.

'Not for a face,' she said. 'That is, not unless you *want* to.'

'What now?'

'Empty your pockets.'

She led him to the Table.

It was one of the big brutes, a Mark J. Surgeon. Suspended over the flat bed was a glittering tangle of probes and pincers and scalpels, springs, clamps and needles. Tubes and looped wires interconnected from one part of the Table to another, crisscrossing the main body which contained the solid-state circuitry forming the machine's memory center and brain. At one end was a console of buttons and switches, lights and dials.

A Table such as this could lengthen bone and change dental patterns. It could broaden shoulders, put on or take off weight. It could alter germ plasm or blood groupings. With its infinitely adjustable lasers it could lay back the flesh surrounding a single nerve and lift out that nerve without nicking the sheath. It was as precise as a diamond cutter and as unemotional as a vending slot.

Logan didn't want to get on the Table. It could carve and change him, make him into another man. Holly 13 fastened down his ankles and wrists, then attached the sensors. The Table rippled, accepted his weight, positioned him.

'I like dark hair,' said Holly, leaning close to him. The blue spark danced in the depths of her eyes. 'Have him give you dark hair.'

Doc returned to his patient. 'Got anything special in mind?' he asked. 'Bone structure like yours I could give you most anything.'

'That's your decision,' snapped Logan. 'Just get it over with.'

'Look, runner,' said Doc, his voice hard, 'just you ease down. I tell you where to go, how to go and *when* to go. You runners are always in a hurry. Always trying to rush me. You don't go nowhere without Doc. I handle this end of things. Can't use the next key anyhow till nine forty. Got plenty of time for the new you.'

Doc danced his fingers over the control board as he studied Logan's face. 'We can widen those cheekbones for a start.'

The Table began to hum as a pair of thin silver probes separated themselves from the overhead cluster and poised above

Logan; a stun needle lowered toward his face; a vibrosaw began to keen.

Abruptly all motion ceased. The keening died. An alarm buzzed insistently.

Doc's eyes narrowed. 'Something's wrong. We've got metal on the Table. You empty your pockets?'

Logan nodded.

Doc looked at him suspiciously. '*Something* ain't right.'

He came out from behind the console, stood over Logan. The slight bulge of the Gun was visible in Logan's waist. Doc pulled open his shirt, baring the weapon.

'Lock the door, Holly.'

'What is it?' she asked, moving forward. Doc shoved her back.

'Gun!' he said. 'We got a Sandman.'

'What'll we do?'

'I'm thinking.' Doc glared at Logan, helpless on the Table.

'You've seen my hand,' said Logan. 'I'm on Lastday. Does it figure I'd still be working for DS?'

'You got a Gun,' said Doc. 'Only DS men got Guns.'

'I'm not the first Sandman to run.'

'Why should I take a chance?' said Doc, moving back to the console. 'I'm scrambling the Table. You'll get more than a new face, Sandman.'

Logan lunged against the straps, but they held fast.

'What will it *do* to him?' asked Holly. The blue light gleamed in her eyes.

'Anything. It's on its own.'

The Table hummed to life.

'I want to watch,' said Holly, flushing.

Doc chuckled.

Logan looked up, sweating, into the moving cluster of pointed, bladed objects suspended above him. A stun needle lanced into his cheek, and the left side of his face went dead. A pair of metal clamps bit into his right leg below the knee. A surgical scalpel slit his shirt from shoulder to waist, leaving a thread of blood in its wake. A sponge dipped to wipe the blood neatly away.

Desperately Logan sucked in his belly and tried to flatten himself into the Table.

Beside him, Holly was breathing fast.

A wide serrated blade shifted its downward sweep, moved three inches to the right and hovered. A pair of nervescissors snipped viciously at empty air, lowered abruptly and sliced through the strap that confined Logan's right arm.

Doc took a shocked step back as Logan clawed the Gun free.

A rain of silver knives dropped toward him, and he hacked at them with the barrel. They snapped like icicles.

Logan attempted to swing the Gun in Doc's direction. 'Kill the Table!'

Lizard-quick, Doc was out the door, the girl behind him.

The Table pumped a cooling alcohol spray on Logan's chest as he clumsily freed his other wrist. Tiny lubricated gears inside the machine's housing slid into new positions.

Logan sprawled the upper part of his body off the bed and hit the leg releases. He rolled from the Table as it mindlessly attacked its own vitals.

It died, shrieking, as sparks showered from the gutted machine.

Logan considered his next move. Without another punch-key, which Doc apparently was to supply, his run was over. And it wouldn't take a mouth like Doc long to spread the word: Sandman. The trail would end before it began.

He kicked the back door open and found himself in a dank warren of intersecting hallways. The moaning cry of the fire-galleries drifted up to him, mixed with the baked desert smell of dreamdust from the hallucimills.

Something iced out of the gray half-darkness, knocking the Gun from his grasp. A glacier numbness chilled his arm from hand to elbow.

Popsickle!

Logan spun into a fighting crouch to face the dim white figure coming at him with the refrigerated police billy held at waist level. Doc, in for the kill.

One blow to the chest and Logan's body would be a sea of

ice crystals, freezing heart action, stopping the breath in his throat. The Gun lay on the floor, rimed with frost.

He kept his eyes locked on the short smoke-colored stick in Doc's practiced hand. The popsickle slashed air as Doc lunged past him. Logan twisted and fell to one knee in the classic Omnite attack position. His left elbow drove into Doc's groin. With a soundless, choked scream, Doc slammed the wall, bouncing off into Logan's knee, which caught him with a killing spinal blow.

Logan swore bitterly, stripping the dead man's pockets. I should have handled this without killing him, he thought. Now where's the next key? Has the girl got it? And where is she? Probably hidden somewhere in the Arcade labyrinth.

Logan retrieved the moist Gun, straightening to a sound in the next room. He moved carefully to the door, easing it open.

Holly was inside, against the far wall, a medical knife poised at her breast. Her terror-glazed eyes were fixed on the Gun. As Logan advanced toward her she drove the blade into her chest.

The world ended abruptly for Holly 13.

Logan put away his weapon.

'Doyle . . . Doyle . . . is that you?' A drugged voice.

Logan stepped through an alum-mesh curtain. The cramped room reeked of anesthetic. A dark-haired girl, nude to the waist, was rising groggily from a pneumocot.

She blinked dreamily at Logan. 'It's me – *Jessica,*' she said; her fingers tentatively explored the new planes of her face.

A runner, thought Logan. Her hand is blinking. But why does she think I'm Doyle? And did she get the –

'Key. Do you have a punchkey?' he asked.

'Doyle . . . you don't look like my brother anymore. You don't even *sound* the same. They've changed us.'

So that was it: the girl was Doyle's sister. He must have told her to meet him here.

'Listen,' said Logan, 'do you have the next key?'

She was fully awake now, slipping into her blouse. He saw her remove a silver object from one pocket. Logan took it from her. A mazekey.

'Did Doc give you any instructions?'

'Yes. He told me – us – to use a branch tunnel under Arcade. I know where it is.'

'All right then. Let's go.'

He followed her to a slideway. They plunged down into jeweled darkness.

At the off ramp he took her hand. They ran along the maze platform.

The maze. A million miles of tunnel, a veining of expressways serving the continents, interlinking Chicago with New York, Detroit with New Alaska, London and Lower Australia – a multitude of black-steel beetles burrowing the subterranean depths at fantastic speeds.

Logan stabbed the mazekey into a callbox at the edge of the platform.

A distant brass humming along the tunnels, a rocketing rush of deep-earth winds; the mazecar blazed out of darkness and socked into the boarding slot.

They climbed in. The hatch slid closed. The seats locked.

'Destination?' asked the car.

Jessica said, 'Sanctuary.'

The mazecar surged into fluid motion.

As the beetle rushed, Logan's thoughts rushed with it. Sanctuary. It seemed too easy; you got into a mazecar and said a word and the obedient piece of machinery carried you – *where?*

And the girl, Jessica? How would he deal with her?

The car slowed, hissed to a stop. The hatch opened.

Jessica didn't move. 'They can change the color of a man's eyes but they can't change the man inside. You're not my brother.'

'He's dead,' Logan told her.

The girl's mouth tightened. 'You killed him.'

'No – but I saw him die. He gave me his key. He – wanted me to have it.'

For a moment her face was still; then she began to sob quietly.

What do you say? How do you say I'm sorry? A Sandman

doesn't feel sorry. He does what he has to.

'Look,' he said. 'Your brother's dead and we're alive. And if we want to stay alive we'll have to keep moving. It's just that simple.'

'Exit, please,' said the car.

They stepped out and the machine whipped away.

The maze platform was lifeless. Dusty yellow sunlight speared down from a jagged hole in the tunnel ceiling. Loose metal tiles lay in disordered heaps where they had sloughed from the walls. Exposed masonry jutted through cracked anodized flooring.

On a rusting section of tunnel wall a weathered poster clung, edges peeling. On it a running silhouette was overprinted with harsh letters: SHAME. Directly under this a vandal had chalked RUNNERS STINK!

A bent sign angled over the platform: *CATHEDRAL.*

And what now? Logan asked himself. Is *this* Sanctuary? A shorted-out section of city swarming with renegade cubs....

'Listen!' Jess warned.

A distant singing. A faint rising and falling refrain, echoing from an upper level.

Logan ducked Jess into a wedge of shadow. They waited.

Faintly: *Sandman, Sandman,*
leave my door.
Don't come back here
any more.

A high, childish treble, coming closer.

'Cubs!' said Logan. His eyes strained the darkness.

Louder: *Now I lay me*
down to pray.
Sandman, Sandman,
stay away....

A small figure in a tattered blue garment walked into the circle of sun on the platform. A little girl of five. She was dragging something behind her. The child's face was grimed and hair-tangled; her scabbed legs were thin. She wore no shoes.

She stopped singing. 'Don't be afraid,' she said. 'I'm Mary-Mary 2.'

Logan stepped from the shadow. 'What are you doing here?'

'Oh, he told me to meet you.'

'Who did?'

The little girl's eyes saucered. 'Why, the old, old man, of course.'

Jessica gripped the child's shoulder. 'What old, old man?'

'His hair is black and white, all mixed together,' she told them. 'And he has deep places in his face and he looks so wise. He's the oldest man in the world.'

'Ballard!'

The little girl took a silver key from a torn pocket. 'He told me to give you this.'

Logan palmed the key. 'Do we use it now?'

'This many,' she said solemnly, raising her tiny hands, all ten fingers spread. In the center of her right palm a yellow flower glowed softly.

'Ten o'clock,' said Jess.

Logan checked a wallchron above them. 'Twelve minutes.'

Jessica looked deeply into the waif's eyes. 'Where do you live, Mary-Mary?'

She smiled. 'Here,' she said.

'Why aren't you in a nursery?'

'I'm very smart,' said Mary-Mary.

'But don't you get hungry?'

'You can catch things to eat.'

She opened the frayed cloth bag at her feet and proudly held out an old-fashioned rat trap. Jessica paled.

'I *never* go upstairs,' continued Mary-Mary. 'The bad people are there and they chase you. Goodbye now! You're a nice old lady.'

The child looked disdainfully at Logan and walked off into the tunnels.

'I don't think she likes me,' he said.

'She shouldn't be here,' said Jess. 'Alone in a place like this. She should be in a nursery with other children.'

'She seems to be self-sufficient.'

'A nursery would protect her.'

'As it protected you?'

'Of course. No child under seven belongs on her own. I was happy in the nursery.' Jess sat down on the platform edge with Logan. 'No, no I wasn't happy.' Her voice trembled. 'I accepted everything then, without questioning – but I was never happy there.'

Logan let the girl talk; he wanted to know more about her, wanted to understand her.

'Why should every child be taken from its parents at birth? Why should a brother and sister be separated for seven years?' She studied Logan's face. 'When did *you* begin to doubt, to question Sleep? I'd like to know.'

'I can't recall just when. I'd heard the stories, of course.'

'Of Ballard?'

'Yes. And the rest of it.'

'About the Sanctuary line. Oh, how I wanted to believe those stories when I first heard them as a little girl.' Her eyes grew hard again. 'Do you ever wonder what your mother was like, who she was, what she felt, how she looked? Do you think she'd be ashamed of what you've become?'

'She may have been a runner, too,' said Logan evasively. 'I'll never know what she was.'

Jess frowned angrily. 'I think you should. I think children *should* know their mothers and be loved by them. Little Mary-Mary should have a mother to love her. A machine can never love you . . . only people can love people.'

'Where did you work before you ran?' he asked her.

'I was a fashion tech at Lifeleather trim. Three hours a day, three days a week. I hated it.'

'Then why did you stay there?'

'Because it was a job. What can anyone really *work* at? You can paint or write poetry or go on pairup. You can glass-dance or firewalk in the Arcades.' Her voice was scornful. 'You can breed roses or collect stones or compose for the Tri-Dims. But there's no meaning to any of it. I just – '

A scream from the tunnels.

'That was Mary-Mary!' Jess lunged forward, but Logan restrained her.

'Wait,' he said. 'Here she comes.'

The child ran out of the darkness into Jessica's arms. 'The *bad* people! Bad, bad, bad!'

A howling group of cubscouts burst from the tunnel mouth to surround them. A strutting, feral-faced thirteen-year-old headed the pack. From the waist up he was dressed in the bloodstained uniform of a DS man. Below the ripped black tunic he wore sweat-darkened skintights. 'Here now and look what Charmin' Billy led you to.' He smirked. 'The little rat-trapper and two stinkin' runners.'

Mary-Mary stomped her foot. 'You go on away!' she demanded. 'This is *my* place. Go back upstairs!'

Charming Billy ignored her. 'Going to have us a time, we are!'

Logan measured the pack with his eyes. He could summon the car in another five minutes. *How do you buy five minutes?* He'd take out the blocky cub to his right first and then go for Charming Billy if nothing else worked. He eased Jess and the child behind him.

Logan looked at Billy. 'I feel sorry for you, boy.'

Confusion. The pack watched their leader.

'For me? Better feel sorry for yourself, Runner!'

'No – for *you*, Billy. How old are you?'

Billy's eyes slitted. He didn't reply.

'Twelve? Thirteen? Now me, I'm as old as you can get.' Logan slowly exposed his blinking timeflower. 'And you – your days are running out. How long can you last, Billy?'

One minute gone.

'Two years? A year? Six months?' he pointed to the blue flower glowing in Billy's palm. 'What happens when you go to red?'

'Got me a Sandman once, I did! They said I'd never get him, but I cut him up good, I did. Make the rules as I go. Cubs do what *I* say. Always have. Always will. I got Cathedral and I'll never let go!'

'No cubs at fourteen, Billy. Ever heard of a cub with a red flower? You'll leave Cathedral then, Billy, when you're on red, because they won't let an adult stay here. The young ones. They'll gut-rip you if you stay, so you'll cross the river. And then, almost before you know it, Billy, you're twenty-one and your hand is blinking. And you'll die like a sheep.'

Two minutes gone.

'Not me, I won't!' Billy shouted. 'I'll – '

' – run!' snapped Logan. 'Isn't that *just* what you'll do? Run as I'm running. As she's running.'

'Shut up! Shut up your damn mouth! I ain't no stinkin' runner!'

'We're the same kind, Billy. You're just like us. Help us, Billy. Don't fight us.'

The blocky cub cut in. 'Let him suck Muscle. That'll shut his mouth. Let's watch him shake himself to death!'

The anger and frustration drained from Charming Billy's face. He smiled.

Logan tensed. The talking was done.

Three minutes gone.

Drugpads materialized. The cubs squeezed the pads, inhaled the Muscle. They shimmered into kaleidoscopic blurs, into weaving color patterns. Here. There. They were everywhere.

Logan fell back into a fighting crouch, but before he could strike a blow he was caught, dragged and slammed against the wall.

Screaming, Mary-Mary broke from Jessica and ran off down the tunnels.

A staccato burst of words; the blocky cub's voice, 'Give-himsomeMuscle!'

'Shakehimtodeath!'

'Killhim!'

A drugpad danced the air in front of Logan's face.

Four minutes gone.

Logan held his breath. The fumes enveloped him; if he breathed. . . . He felt the Gun pressing into his thigh. The *Gun.*

Despite revealing himself to Jess, he'd have to use the Gun.

He wrenched his arms loose, dropped to the floor, rolled free of the weaving shapes, drew and fired.

The nitro charge exploded into the pack. Fragmented bodies littered the platform.

Five minutes!

Logan quickly pocketed a drugpad and keypunched the callbox.

Jess stared at him with revulsion. 'Sandman! You're a *Sandman!*'

A mazecar swooped out of the depths.

'In!'

Jessica hesitated. Logan pushed the girl inside, leaped after her. Before the hatch could engage a black shimmer filled the space.

The shimmer solidified into Charming Billy.

He was headless.

The hatch shut.

The mazecar slammed into night.

8

A light flares.

He smiles. Logan's Gun has been fired.

He notes the coordinates. They pinpoint a spot beneath the dead area of Cathedral.

He goes there.

He examines the bodies on the platform.

He picks up a used Muscle pad, flings it away.

He examines the callbox, probes at the terminals. Logan has taken a mazecar.

He frowns darkly.

He hears a faint child's voice singing, 'Sandman, Sandman, leave my door. . . .'

The voice fades.

He follows the sound down the tunnel.

NIGHT . . .

AT THE END OF THE TWENTIETH CENTURY, before the Little War, when men spawned like microbes on a culture dish, the great problem was food. The fourth horseman rode the land and his name was Famine.

Man reached for the planets and found them puddled gas and frozen stone. He reached for the stars and was driven back by $E = mc^2$ – and he abandoned space.

There was the sea. Six-sevenths of the world. A wave rises in a ripple and marches in growing kinetic motion for thousands of wet miles to smash on continental shores. That is the *surface* of the sea. Beneath the surface: the Depths. Light filters slowly down into murky dimness for the first hundred feet. Lower still, and light is dead. Only darkness remains. Pressures and swift currents and yeasty life mix in a savage broth.

And far below, where reinforced steel acts like balsa, and nightmare creatures carry their own light, is Molly, once queen of the teeming sea.

She took an age to build. She covered a hundred undersea miles. She provided living quarters and work space for twenty thousand technicians and their families – and she gave sustenance to a quarter of the world. She was a vast food-processing center sunk under a plasteel dome, and through her locks came subs and tenders, skimmers and harvesters.

Protein is protein whether it is obtained from a steer or a squid. With the proper mixture of carbohydrates, vitamins, minerals, the protein molecule can be made into any foodstuff, and the protein molecule lives in a million forms in the sea.

Molly showed the way. After her they built the Zuther-Notion, the Proteus and Manta City. But Molly was the queen.

Until 6:03 P.M. Common Standard Time, March 6, 2033. At that moment intolerable pressures in the Challenger Deep, acting through uncounted centuries, caused a tenth of an inch slippage along two fault planes crossing the Marianas Trench – and a hairline crack appeared in Molly's plasteel dome. A solid bar of water knifesliced through seven levels, destroying a hundred compartments in one insane instant. Molly screamed. Steel tore like paper. Fourteen thousand men, women and children mixed their atoms with the sea in the first chaotic shock.

Molly absorbed the blow. Pressures equalized; bulkheads strained, tore, accepted the load, howled as the ocean tide-tons bent them inward. Automatic valves closed; hatches slammed. In twelve seconds she was a jumbled conglomerate of corpses, of flooded compartments and corridors, of machinery, jack-straw-heaped. But she held.

Some of her compartments retained air – and against these watertight chambers the sea gnawed with a patient gnawing that would never stop until Molly was completely dead.

She had begun her long war with the sea.

The mazecar slotted into Molly. The seats unlocked.

'Exit, please.'

Jessica didn't resist as Logan guided her through the hatch.

The platform, buried in greenblack fathoms, creaked and shifted, shifted and creaked beneath them. The great surging skin of the Pacific pressured in against the bubbleglass. The air held an odor of iron and age, a smell of medicated wounds. A dull booming, far off. Echoes. Silence.

Why here, under the sea? wondered Logan. Who was the next contact?

The girl looked vacant, dead. Hatred burned in Jessica, deeply, but the will to resist had left her.

'All right,' said Logan. 'So I've got a DS Gun. And, back in my unit, I've got a black tunic to match it. But now I'm a runner. Just as you are.'

'Sandmen don't run,' she said flatly.

'And Sandmen don't eat. And Sandmen don't breathe. And Sandmen don't get tired. Well, *I'm* tired. I'm tired and I'm hungry and I'm sick of being jumped and kicked at and hated.'

She looked at him coldly. 'You're a monster. You've chased and killed people like my brother, whose only sin was wanting to live another day.'

'I didn't kill your brother.'

'Maybe not, but you *would* have. You'd have put a homer

in him and been proud of yourself for doing it.'

He had no answer.

Jess drew in a ragged breath. '*Damn* you!' she flared. 'You DS live by pain, by hurting and wounding and killing. You destroy in the name of mass survival and you never think about the sick wrongness of it, the horror of it. . . . You enjoy using the Gun and you burn with it and you terrorize with it! Damn your kind and damn your system! You're a foul, rotten – '

Logan slapped her hard across the cheek to stop the words which cut him like stones.

She put up a shaking hand to the drop of blood at the corner of her mouth.

Her flower was charcoal.

'It's changed,' said Logan. 'You're on *black*.' His hand automatically drifted toward the warm pearl handle of the Gun.

The girl looked at him in horror.

Logan hesitated.

He had taken on the shape and coloration and mental attitudes of a runner, and it was impossible for him to know where the dividing line really was.

In that suspended moment, Jessica wheeled off down the long platform.

'Jess!'

The girl ran.

She ran as a deer in panic runs, heedlessly, blindly, driven forward by the desire to put distance between herself and the hunter. A spiral of metal steps carried her upward; her feet rattled against metal cleats, leaving an echo path for Logan to follow.

She pounded along a narrow culture corridor lined with flashing sea life. Squid and porpoise and eel, shark and barracuda and the trunkback turtle marked her passage. Ahead of her the corridor dead-ended at a tall durasteel door controlled by a bar of chilled iron. Jess threw herself at the bar, tugging, dragging her body's weight against it.

The bar moved slightly.

A dry-grass hiss, a rush of heat – and, just one inch from Jessica's head, an armored steg harpoon buried itself in the steel door.

'Wait up there, girl! Open *that* hatch, and the sea will take us both.'

Standing wide-legged, holding a primed steglauncher in two bloated hands, was an incredible figure. Hormones had gone wild in him; a rampaging thyroid had built a giant. His bristled head brushed the corridor ceiling. An oiled slicker the color of midnight draped his swollen frame. His face was a moon.

His name was Whale.

'Look out!' Jess pointed down the corridor at Logan.

Whale billowed about. Seeing the Gun in Logan's belt, his eyes vanished in moonflesh. The steglauncher fixed its metal eye on Logan's stomach. 'What's this? Told to wait for two runners, and what do I get? Runner don't chase a runner.'

'He's with DS,' snapped Jess.

Whale considered this placidly. A sudden thudding in the depths of the bubble city; another collapsing bulkhead. Whale flinched, his great mass rippling.

'I'm a runner,' said Logan. 'I tried to tell her, but she wouldn't believe me.'

'So why should *I*?' asked Whale quietly. He held up a thick hand, opened sausage fingers. A charcoal flower was lost in folded flesh. The steglauncher did not waver.

Anger and frustration clouded Logan's mind. Anything he said could kill him.

'Just you ease out that Gun and put it on the deck, my lad,' rumbled Whale.

With the deliberate control of a glassdancer, Logan placed the Gun on the floor, eyes never leaving the cold bore of the steglauncher which moved to cover him.

He straightened.

'Now,' said Whale, 'let's us all take a little march through Molly.'

He herded them back down the corridor.

'You drylanders don't know about Molly. She's a real fighter, she is. She's like me. She don't die easy.'

Up the slanting wall of a slimed compartment, along a twisting catwalk suspended over blackness, through a beamed jungle of ripped and bent conveyors acrid with the smell of spilled oil and brine. Crab creatures scuttled at their approach; phosphor fish darted in shallow bilgewater as the three figures corkscrewed down through the dying bubble city.

The water climbed their legs until it took them at thigh level. Whale undogged a final beaded bulkhatch and pushed Logan through ahead of him. Wet tonnages drummed the chamber. In this small coffin space the ocean was a living presence; the sledging boom of iced undersea tides quaked the walls, and dust powdered down in damp brown showers.

Without the Gun, and under the implacable eye of the weapon in Whale's hand, Logan felt powerless.

'She's sick down here,' said Whale. 'Fightin' hard, she is.' Shifting the launcher, he placed a gentle hand against the pitted metal of the wall. 'Hold on, Molly girl,' he crooned. 'Ya showed 'em what ya got. I know you're hurt. You've taken all the sea can give. Hold! I've brought ya help.'

He fixed Logan with his eyes. 'If you wanta live, mate, you'll help Molly fight her battle. Just put your weight to that wall.'

The mountain of man squeezed back, out of the chamber.

'When the bulkhead goes, you go with it.'

'Wait,' cried Jess. She blocked the hatch. 'You're not leaving him *here*?'

Whale rumbled. 'Where else? Molly needs him.'

'But then you're no better than he is. A killer.'

'A man kills to save himself.' He brushed her aside, slamming the hatch and dogged it.

Outside, he handed her a key. 'Use this at ten forty for the next car. And you'd better step. You know where the landing is.'

Jess looked at him, white-faced.

A dull reverberation trembled the floorplates.

'Molly's callin' and I got work to do. Tell Ballard we're

still holdin'.'

And, with amazing agility, he weaved through a thicket of spars and stanchions to disappear into Molly's vitals.

In the sweating dark, Logan felt despair. His last hope was gone. He was dead and he knew it. Now he felt as a runner feels, feared as a runner fears.

He traced the sweep of flexing coffin with searching fingers. No openings. Nothing to use on the hatch. Why hadn't he taken his chances against the harpoon? It ripped your gut out, but at least it was quick. Not like this. A place like this could break a man's courage, stretch his nerve, unman him.

Well, I'm getting what I asked for, he thought. And maybe I deserve it for what I've done. God, maybe I do. So let the damn sea have me.

Logan fought a sudden urge to smash at the walls.

The Pacific leaned its weight against the chamber; water dripped continually, increasing in volume. Logan was chest deep in the cold tide. It rose toward his chin; he clamped his mouth shut. The chamber groaned under immense pressures.

Then abruptly the hatch opened. The water receded. Jess was there.

'Quick,' she said. 'There's not much time.'

In subsector 8, section T, level zero, now completely submerged, a tiny crustacean burrowed a hundredth of an inch further into a conduit, since it was the creature's nature to burrow. The tiny crawler blazed into blue-white heat.

In callbox 192978-E a micro terminal rose seven and a half degrees, shorting out a relay. A wire-cluster fused, and a new circuit was born.

'Sanctuary,' they had said to the mazecar.

But it did not take them to Sanctuary.

Instead, it took them to Hell.

7

He examines the data.

Fact: Doyle 10 *had a sister, Jessica* 6.

Fact: Jessica 6 *is on Lastday.*

Fact: His interrogation of the little girl, Mary-Mary 2, *has revealed that Logan is with Jessica.*

He watches the board. It is silent, dark. No lights glow. No needles quiver.

The maze scanners are silent, dark.

The Gun tracer is silent, dark.

The Follower is silent, dark.

Impossible.

His quarry has vanished.

LATE NIGHT . . .

HELL: NAMED AFTER THE ANCIENT religious concept of eternal punishment. Over a thousand miles of dead glare-ice wilderness between Baffin Bay and the Bering Sea. A sharded tumble of floes and bergs and nightmare crevasses, of daggered ice cliffs and howling glacial frost winds. A crippling, killing, freezing, forsaken world of white on white on white.

Hell: fourteen burrows in an irregular semicircle on the lee side of a storm-carved berg. Each cramped ice cell clawed from the iron surface by dying, lonely men and women working in subzero cold. Near the entrance to one hide-hole was a rich red stain on the ice glass, where an unknown convict had lung-hemorrhaged under the refrigerated glare of the midnight sun.

The maelstrom of cold had shaped a ledge into a stubby pedestal, and topping the pedestal was a hand-hewn ice block. Within that transparent mass a dark shape swam in frozen silence.

There were no guards. Nor were they needed.

No man ever walked out of Hell.

When Logan and Jess arrived, an alarm sounded. The platform itself dealt with them. They were needlestunned, packaged and conveyed through a force field labyrinth and dumped on the ice.

The platform had disappeared. There was no way back.

Warden came to meet them. A man hunched against driving wind, a fur-shrouded scarecrow. His feet were rag-wrapped, his face old leather and iodine; his eyes burned under a filth-stiffened parka.

He bent over their cocooned figures and his mittened hands clumsily stripped away the con-webbing. Wadding the precious material, he thrust it into his parka.

Cold clubbed them.

Logan stumbled up, pulling Jess with him. In the severe cold the effects of the needle drug were rapidly dissipated.

'Wh – where's the key?' he asked Warden. This man must be their contact.

'When you come to Hell they throw away the keys.'

Logan felt the brass taste of fear in his mouth. They were in the escape-proof prison city at the North Pole.

'Come learn the rules,' said Warden. He turned his back and paced off across the glare sheet.

They struggled after him. The wind died to a low snarl as they reached the partial shelter of the great iceberg which loomed over the burrows.

'Your neighbors,' said Warden.

Fur-swaddled figures surrounded them, emerging in clots of twos and threes from the ink-mouthed holes. Logan scanned the emaciated, skull-haunted faces that hedged him in a wolf circle.

'Rule one,' said Warden. 'A new convict can pick his antagonist. Two: the antagonist can use any weapon he has to defend himself and his goods. Three: the new man fights barehanded. That's all the rules we got – except winner gets first cut.'

'And if I don't fight?' asked Logan.

'Then ya die on the ice,' said Warden. 'Course, that don't go for the girl.' He grinned. 'And ya better get to it. Couple minutes more out here, dressed like you are, and you won't *need* to choose.'

Under the wind's hammer, Logan's clothing was gauze. He measured the corded figures, looking for weakness and found none. These were survivors. No soft ones here.

He pointed a random finger. 'Him,' said Logan.

The circle tightened to take up the slack left by the man who stepped forward. Tall. Long-armed. Thick-shouldered. From the matted fur at his chest he drew forth a needle-pointed stiletto of hand-burnished ice. Eight inches of lethal blade, shaped with an artist's care.

Instantly he lunged. The stiletto flashed. He had led with the knife. Logan took advantage of this mistake to chop the weapon from his hand. It shattered on the ice, but Logan's foot slid on one of the shards and he was down, the man atop him, hands at his throat.

Logan felt the sinewed fingers close on his windpipe.

He broke the chokehold and the man's neck with one blow.

Warden looked stunned and disappointed. The circle of eyes shifted hungrily to the dead body, already frost-dusted. Now they moved in to strip the clothing, which they piled at Logan's feet. The corpse was hustled away.

'That was Harry 7 you just took care of,' said Warden. 'Pick up his clothes and claim his goods.' Warden walked to the mouth of a burrow. 'This hide-hole's yours. Harry didn't have no woman. You share everything with the girl.'

Logan followed Jess into the narrow, fetid mouth of the ice cave. Inside, they hurriedly donned the evil-smelling hides of Harry 7. The temperature was twenty degrees warmer, but it was still chillingly cold.

They sat down together on a thin layer of shredded con-webbing which had been spread against the ice. Logan pressed close to Jess. She withdrew, her face set.

Well, here we go again, he thought angrily. She knew he'd had no choice out there. She was alive in the clothes of a dead man, but she couldn't accept the fact that he had to kill to get them.

'I listened to you as we were coming into the platform,' he said. 'I hid the Gun so the contact wouldn't connect me with DS. With the Gun we'd have some kind of a chance here. But we don't. And right now you need me a lot more than I need you.'

After a moment he felt her settle against him. 'What are we going to do?' she asked.

'Nothing. Until we know more.'

A scuffling sound at the entrance. Warden appeared.

'Come see Black Tom.'

They followed him out. Warden led them for a short distance across the blowing ice.

'Here he is.' Warden gestured theatrically.

They looked up at the dark shape in the transparent block above them. Inside the ice was *part* of a man.

He had no legs. One of his arms was a flat, paddle-shaped stump. The remaining arm arched forward, terminating in taloned fingers. All the fat was gone, and the bone structure was exposed in raw relief. The arm strained in a bowed curve, clawing for life. Nestled against the shoulder was the head. Staring out of a twisted visage were eyes of milk. Wind and sun and wilderness had carved him.

He was black.

'He was a white man, once,' said Warden.

Jessica looked away.

'Black Tom's up there for a reason,' Warden went on. 'He ain't what you'd call decoration. You can learn from Tom. He cracked the two-year mark in Hell. He watched 'em come and he watched 'em go – until he went snowblind the end of the first year. A month later frostbite got his legs, but that didn't slow him. He dug two burrows by hisself to keep his place, and tanned the skins you're wearin' on your backs. They say he bit his arm off when an ice slide trapped him. Anyhow, he come in without it. Tom lived longest 'cause he learned fastest.' Warden spat on the ice. 'Me, I've lasted more'n a year already – and there's none here can say the same. Do like you're told, and you may last the week.'

'Savage!' flamed Jess. 'Why do you live like this?'

Warden's reply was edged. 'Living's better than dying.'

'You could cooperate,' she said. 'You could work together instead of *slaughtering* each other.'

'Work for what?'

'Food, clothing, tools. . . .'

'There's damn little food, less clothing and no tools. It takes wood and stone and metal to build something, and the only metal around here is in Box.'

A man loped up to drop a soggy bundle at their feet. 'Here's your cut,' the man said to Logan.

He picked up the bundle – and unwrapped the liver and heart of Harry 7! Jess stepped back with a look of horror. Logan dropped the bundle; it stained the snow.

'We don't waste food here,' snapped Warden. 'This ain't a threemile complex in Nebraska. Now pick up your share. When you get hungry enough you'll eat it.'

'There must be other food,' said Logan.

'Out there.' Warden swept the lifeless horizon with his hand. 'Maybe a mile, maybe a hundred. If you're lucky you'll stumble across a seal whelp, which ain't very likely. Black Tom killed a penguin once with an ice spear. We lost three men last month, tryin' to pull down a bull seal – and Redding lost all his fingers. Ice too thick to reach the fish if there is any. And if you don't have luck in the first hour there ain't a second. Shackelford made himself a slingshot outa hide strips, but he froze solid before he could use it. Sure, there's food. There's polar bear and ptarmigan, teal and otter, and you're welcome to hunt 'em down, if you can find 'em. And when you do they can hide better, run faster and jump quicker than you can. I tell you this – go join Box out there if you don't care for the table we set.'

'Box? Who's he?'

'Box ain't a he. He's a *what*.'

Logan looked curiously at Warden.

'Maybe he's got a name, but I don't know it,' said Warden. 'He got chewed up in a belt jump after a torture jig with a ten-year-old. The gears scattered him some. He was half dead then, but the system don't let go that easy. They sewed him back together, and what they couldn't find they *made*. After they was done they put him on a Hellcar. He lit out soon as he got here, and he's a hard one to find.

'One thing I'll say for him. He must know where the food is and how to get it. If you can catch him maybe you can make him show you. You might try up north, about two miles, near the cliffs.' He grinned wolfishly. 'But you can bet he won't be waitin' there for you.'

'We'll risk it,' said Logan.

'Then go,' said Warden. 'You won't be comin' back.'

When they stepped from the shelter of the berg, the wind took them.

Box lived in a white world. He moved in storms of dusted ice and loneliness. He did not tire; he was never cold; a part of him never slept. His world was porcelain and pale marble, alabaster and bone ivory. He made castles of bergs and palaces of glacier cliffs. He cloud-wandered the frozen immensities.

And was content.

Box saw them coming: two staggering figures, bent against the wind. He vanished.

Logan fought the clogging exhaustion in his body. The wind leaped in to snatch his breath, battered his face and hands, rip-sawed through his furred clothing. The dreaming cliffs on the ice-dazzled plain were no closer. They would never be closer. They were ten thousand miles away. They were an illusion which stung him forward, one leaden foot after the other leaden foot after the other leaden foot after the other leaden foot after the other leaden foot. . . .

Jessica toppled and fell.

He pulled at her, tugging at an arm. No going forward. No going back. No more steps. The cliffs were dream and dream; they had never existed. Logan slipped down beside Jess. Her eyes were closed. She should open her eyes, he thought lazily. She'll die. If she does not open her eyes she'll die and that would be too bad. Too bad.

If *I* close my eyes, he thought, I can open them again immediately. There will be no problem in this. Close. Open. No problem. I would tell her to open her eyes, but I will save this for later and show her how easy it is to open and close your eyes.

Logan closed his eyes.

He would open them in a moment, in just another moment after a moment and then he would tell Jess and would open them and in a moment he would and it was so easy to keep them closed for a moment and the wind had gone and that was strange and there was no cold and he could open them in a moment and there was no problem and he would. He would.

Logan slept.

He opened his eyes to a frieze of crystal beasts dancing in a blue fire. He blinked. The frieze wavered, became solid. Extending to the limit of his vision was a capering host of otters conjured from diamond ice. And more.

Logan sat up to an incredible tableau.

There, a fish of sequined rainbow scales caught in a zircon wave.

There, a tusked walrus with mirror-ice eyes, his body veined with blacks and purples.

There, a flight of crystal birds in a crystal sky.

Planes and projections. An intricate scrimshaw of glassed fretwork, rising in prismed tiers, shot through with light jewels: dandelion yellows, crimson lakes, cerulean blues, flashing and reflecting, illuminated by a barrel-sized lamp of carved bone which sizzled and flickered. And supporting this fragile lacework was an immense column, angling up into the vaulted roof of the ice cavern.

Logan felt bottled in the heart of a teardrop chandelier.

The room reeked of burning seal oil.

Jess lay on the floor beside him. Her eyes stirred. She awakened, gasped.

'Overwhelming, isn't it?' said a fluting voice.

A creature stood before them on chromed legs. From the midpoint of his sternum to his hips he was coils and cables. One hand was a cutting tool. His head was half flesh, half metal.

'A machine!' said Jess.

'No! not machine, nor man, but a perfect fusion of the two and better than either. You see before you the consummate artist whose magnificent creativity flows from manmetal. The man conceives in hunger and passion; the metal executes with micrometric exactitude. No human sculptor could match the greatness here displayed.'

So this was Box: an insane half-man living in a self-created world of fantasy. Logan wondered just how much humanity remained in him. 'We were told you could help us find food.'

'Dolts!' shrilled Box. 'Barbarians! Are you no more than walking bellies?'

'We're human and we're hungry,' snapped Logan. 'Don't you eat?'

'I feed the soul, not the body. Art before hunger!'

Jessica's eyes ranged about the glittering chamber. 'All of this – it *is* beautiful,' she said softly.

Half of Box smiled. 'Ah – but wait for the winds.' His voice hushed. 'Then my birds sing. My great walrus breathes. My palace chimes and bells. And the deep grottoes whisper my name: Box . . . Box . . . *Bahhhhhxxxsss*.' His voice sobbed into silence.

'Birds, fish, animals . . .' said Jess, with a note of wonder. 'They're all here.'

'Yes, all the creatures. Except Man.' Box scowled. 'They chase me. They want my metal. How they'd love to pry me apart and build a stove from my heart! My legs would make fine knives, fishhooks, spears. But they are blind moles who trip and stumble. I've seen their stiffening bodies on the ice. Worthless. Ugly. Wind-warped. But now – I have found *you*. New ones. Fresh ones. Lovely ones. Suitable models for my masterwork. You will pose for me!'

'If we pose, do we get food?' asked Logan.

'I have no food.'

'Then why should we do it?'

'*Why?* Do you know how long this temple will last? Not twenty-one years, or twenty-one thousand years – but twenty-one thousand thousand years! And you'll be a part of it, the crown jewel in my collection. Ages will roll. Milleniums. And you'll be here – the two of you – eternally frozen in a lovers' embrace.'

Logan turned away.

Box became apprehensive; his voice took on a wheedling tone. 'What can I give you?'

'Nothing,' said Logan. 'We need two things, food and a way out. You have no food, and there's no way out.'

'Ah, but there *is*,' tempted Box.

'Then why are you still here? Why don't you escape?'

'And leave my white wonderland, leave the singing winds and the silence, the purity, the flowing skies . . . For what? For your squabble and smoke, your jamming and rushing? No. But I could. I *could* leave if I wished to do so.'

'How?' asked Logan.

'How indeed,' silked Box. 'First you pose, then I tell you.'

'First you tell us, *then* we pose.'

Box hesitated. Gears seemed to click in him. He moved his metal hand in a gesture of surrender. 'I suppose I must trust you,' he said.

Will he do it? Logan wondered. *Can* he do it? Can he really provide an escape route?

Box put his hand to the metal of his head and closed his human eye. He spoke of visions: 'I am humming in blackness. Far away. I am ten billion, billion neurons in a mighty brain. A brain of steel . . . I am the force that rules the maze.'

The Thinker! It tied in; being half machine, Box was, in a very real sense, part of the great machine brain.

'Above me – a great warrior astride the world. A sweep of black mountain below, great birds on my granite shoulders, a vastness beneath me. I am part of Tashunca-uitco.'

Crazy Horse!

'I am brother to the Thinker,' went on Box. 'I know its circuits and its ways. I share its great wisdom. I can thread the force field labyrinth. I can leave Hell. . . .'

And he told them the way.

Box opened his eye, advanced. 'Now, you shall keep your bargain.'

'How do you want us?' asked Logan.

'Nude,' said Box.

'Take off your clothes,' Logan told Jess, beginning to strip off his own.

The girl looked at him.

'It'll be all right,' he assured her.

Jess pushed back the cowl of her parka and began to unknot the leather ties. She dropped the rank fur at her feet. Averting her eyes from Logan, she touched the magnetic closure on her blouse. It opened under her fingers and she removed the blouse, then quickly peeled away the clear cosmetic supports from her full breasts. Her skirt was added to the clothing on the fur-rich floor. She unzipped her shoes and stepped out of them.

'Enchanting,' said Box.

He waved them to a dais covered with deep white polar furs. 'Up there,' he said.

'Shall we – just *stand*?' asked Jess. 'Or should we. . . .'

'Take her in your arms,' Box said.

Logan looked at Jessica. Lamplight played along the creamed curves and valleys of her body. Her skin was glowing ivory in the light of the flame.

'Stop wasting my time,' Box said. He stood poised at a tall monolith of sparkling ice.

Logan took the girl clumsily into his arms.

'No, no, no,' complained Box. 'With emotion. With feeling. She is your love, your life.' To the girl, he said, 'Mold yourself to his strong body. Look into his eyes.'

Jess looked into Logan's eyes.

He felt the sweet warmth of her, the nearness of her. Breasts pressing him, legs touching him, arms holding him. He felt a slow surge of passion, but more than passion: a rapture, a tenderness, and a wild, sweet sadness he'd never known.

'Superb!' said Box.

His metal hand began to buzz. He brought it forward to shiver the ice into blue patterns. He worked furiously, with incredible speed. In a shower of tinkling shards and ice splinters, the two figures began to emerge from the block. Magically, forming, shaping. . . .

Logan held Jess. This, too, was a house of glass – but how different from the frantic, empty pursuit of sensation in the houses of the city. There was a reality here, a meaning. Forget everything else; forget the twisted man-thing carving the ice; forget the Hell-huddle of convicts; forget Francis and Ballard and the maze and Sanctuary. But let this moment last. *Jess . . . Jess. . . .*

'Done!' piped Box. 'Behold!' He stepped back.

Logan reluctantly released the girl.

They faced *themselves.*

In stunningly wrought ice figures, shimmering with life, the artist had captured the form, the mood, the emotion of his models. The endless moment was there. Love. Passion. Beauty. All there.

Logan forced the image from his mind. They had to move, to dress, to make their escape. No time for love. Or passion. Or beauty. No time.

He turned to reach for his clothing.

And did not anticipate the ripping blow that snuffed out the world.

The world was reborn in a voice that said, 'Torture is also a fine art and I am its master. Your death, my lady, shall be exquisite.'

Logan swam up through fog and froth to full awakening.

He was in an ice cage, behind ice bars. Directly in front of the cage Jess was spread-eagled and helpless, pinned, naked, to a tilted slab. Her body was trembling with chill. Facing her was a steeply inclined slideway. Balanced delicately on the high lip of the slide was a massive ten-ton ice block. An oil flame ate steadily at one end of the great block. Water dripped into white fur.

With each passing second, as more of the ice melted, the end of the block lightened, tipping the remainder. Already the mass was inching over in a continuous grinding crunch, pulled by the slow force of gravity. When enough of it had turned to water the huge block would tip into the slideway and begin its ponderous rush toward Jess. It would bear down with all of its tonnage, like a giant sledge, and the vulnerable body of the girl would be caught between the ice faces as they smashed together.

On the polar-covered dais Box sat, his chromed legs folded beneath him. 'Beg me,' he crooned. 'I can still save your life. Entreat me. Plead with me. Tell me how much you want to live.'

Jess remained silent, her eyes glazed with fright.

Logan threw himself at the bars. They held. Embedded in one of them, midway up, he saw the curved darkness of a small fish, frozen there.

His glance swept the cell. His shirt had been thrown in one corner. Hurriedly he scooped it up and wound it three times around his right hand.

Box was still urging the girl to beg for her life.

The block tipped further.

Logan faced the imperfection in the cell bar, stiffening his fingers into a slight curve, bunching the pad of muscle in the heel of his hand. He assumed the Omnite stance.

Now.

He summoned tension into his body, feeling it gather along the backs of his legs; he felt his spine arch as the muscles pumped full of blood. He concentrated on the hand. He was *only* a hand. He took several deep breaths, let his attention widen to include a spot in space three inches beyond the bar. He would hit *that* spot.

He blanked out the cell bar that was between the spot and his hand. It didn't exist; there *was* no cell bar. He tensed. Energy sang into the arm that slashed the rigid hand at the spot in the air.

A splintering crack. The bar exploded. Logan squeezed through the opening.

He scooped up one of Jessica's shoes and leaped onto the slideway. Ignoring the poised juggernaut at his back, he attacked the ice shackles that held the girl's wrists and feet. Four quick hammer blows and she was free.

Jess screamed. A great rumble at the tip of the slide. The block was loosed. Logan pushed her ahead of him, diving from the slideway just as the awesome masses mated in demolition. Ice dust powdered the air.

An angry buzz of metal. Logan swung around to see Box coming at him.

'Grab your clothes and get out!' he yelled to Jess – and she obeyed him.

Box hurtled in, his half-face contorted with rage and frustration. Logan ducked under the sweep of his cutting hand, which ripped into the room's central pillar. The buzzing metal cut deeply into the column before Box could free it.

Logan fell back, calculating. The love statue: he and Jess in a perfect world, forever locked in sweet embrace. He would have to destroy it, destroy *himself*. Logan wedged his shoulder against his ice thigh and pushed. The statue tilted, rocked, and toppled into the weakened pillar.

A crack fissured the vault.

Logan ran.

Birds showered from the crystal sky. Otters squealed and splintered. The walrus reared. Box died with one maniacal metal cry.

In that single cataclysmic death, the ice creatures cracked and clattered, mirror-smashed in a fractured tumble of shelves and ledges and crystal lace, disintegrated in shimmering waves as the great palace pulled itself down in a blue ruin.

Logan did precisely as Box had instructed. Leading Jess, he was threading the force field labyrinth. Wind chopped and cut at them on the open plain.

To Logan the spot seemed identical with the stormswept terrain that surrounded it. Ice flurries whipped about them as they moved: two steps forward, a step to the right . . . It was hopeless; Box had lied.

They took three paces in a weaving pattern. Angled right, then left. Three more steps forward, one back.

Magic!

They were out – standing on the warm platform.

Hell was gone.

They discarded the filthy pelts.

'Can you get a mazecar?' asked Jess.

'The Gun first,' said Logan. He recovered it from a niche in the side of the platform, checked it. Five charges left: tangler, vapor, ripper, needler and homer.

Logan pried open the back of the callbox and began to shift the terminals.

A car came humming.

'Where now?' the girl asked him.

'To the Black Hills of the Dakotas,' he said. 'Ballard knows how to control the maze. He directs these cars as he needs them. If we want to find him we go to the source. We go to the Thinker.'

6

He is a violence, contained.

He sits in front of the board.

He has not eaten.

He has not slept.

Technicians avoid him, say nothing to him.

His eyes suddenly flash to the board. Brightness there. One of the scanners has registered the presence of a runner.

Location: South Dakota, the Black Hills.

He feels elation.

The hunt resumes.

EARLY MORNING . . .

WHEN CRAZY HORSE MOUNTAIN WAS dedicated the great mass of granite became the site of a monumental project which was to consume half a century. An Indian warrior, 563 feet high and 641 feet long, would ride the land, carved from six million tons of Dakota stone. A mountain would become a man, towering above black-forest wilderness, dwarfing the giant heads of Rushmore.

The sculptor was Korczak Ziolkowski, and under his direction 150,000 tons of rock would be ripped away each year to form his dream. After a decade, more than a million tons of living granite lay in rubble at the foot of the looming mountain – and the feather of the great War Chief of the Ogallala Sioux began to emerge. Obsessed by his vision, Ziolkowski ranged the continents, prying money from the pockets of the rich, the vain, the titled – which he spent on blasting powder, dynamite, cordite, tools, winches and rope.

The work went on. Gradually the mountain sheared away. Nations threw their combined resources behind it, fired by the dramatic image of a great fighting chieftain on a wild-maned stallion. Thousands of laborers and artists toiled on the flanks of the plunging horse. Diamond drillbits and jackhammers tore at the granite heart of the mountain.

And, with infinite slowness, the mammoth figure took its place against the Dakota sky: Tashunca-uitco. Crazy Horse. The ruthless Indian genius who directed the annihilation of Custer's Seventh on the Little Big Horn.

The world marveled.

On an April afternoon, three years before the project's completion, a thick-waisted laborer named Balder 'Bid Ed' Thag was clearing brush on the east flank of Crazy Horse. He was attracted to a cleft in the rocks by a strange, ululating sound; a wind was issuing from the interior of the mountain.

Thag stepped to the wide opening and peered within. The wind slammed him with such force that he had to brace his legs to keep from being pushed off the slope.

Unfortunately for Thag, it was exactly 4:27 o'clock. The banshee wind whistle abruptly stopped. There was a moment of absolute stillness. Then the wind resumed, but this time it was not blowing outward. The wind sucked *in* with irresistible force. It was Thag's misfortune that he was braced in the wrong direction. He lost his footing and toppled into the hole and fell as a stone falls down a well.

The mountain was breathing, but Thag was not.

Many years passed before the Crazy Horse Caverns were discovered again.

Etched by moving water through eons of time from the limestone basement of the mountain chain, they proved to be the most extensive network of cave formations in the world. Beside them, Carlsbad was a worm crawl.

In Custer, South Dakota, the car told Logan and Jess, 'You are entering resistricted territory. I am not permitted to proceed farther.'

At dawn they left the maze and began to trek overland.

In a deep ravine flanking Crazy Horse Mountain was a white metal post. On it a stamped sign.

ABSOLUTELY NO TRESPASSING BEYOND
THIS POINT
DEATH!
KEEP OUT!
U.S. GOVERNMENT

Hidden in the scrub growth: a stubby bark-colored pedestal. And on the ridge, another. And another after that. Linking this progression was a beam of invisible light.

A dappled fawn moved from cover and, with delicate steps, advanced up the ravine. Its nose tested the morning air for danger and found none.

It breasted the beam.

On the high granite shoulders of Crazy Horse, bronze feathers stirred. Circuits clicked.

The questing fawn lowered its sun-warmed head to lap softly at clear water in a natural stone basin. It did not see the two shadows which hushed over evergreen country. It did not see the two gold shapes which came out of the sun.

Hooded jewel eyes. Razored talons. A cruel hook of steel beak. Assassins.

The mech eagles struck.

A bloodrag of fur lay on the forest floor.

Logan looked up at the sign. 'We're almost there.'

'It says "Death." ' Jessica hesitated.

'Keep moving,' he told her. The Gun was in his hand.

In cloud fastness the mech eagles drifted down the sloped sky, their twenty-foot wings spread against the cushioning air. Currents buoyed the metal bodies in their glide and circle; photo-electric eyes locked on the two toiling ant figures far below.

A copper command in skullcase metal: *Kill!*

They dived.

In that last instant Logan saw them coming. He smashed Jess to the ground, rolling over her. And took the blow. Blinding pain raked his back. Three deep furrows from shoulder to hip welled blood and torn cloth. Through a pain mist he fumbled in the brush for the fallen Gun.

Sun blazed on climbing gold. The birds wheeled and came back. *Kill!*

Logan's enemy fingers clawed at the Gun in the tangle of root grass. He could not get hold of it. He dug and scrabbled at it. Blinking back waves of pain, he gripped the barrel. He juggled it around awkwardly, and his two hands closed on the pearl handle. He had it now. He bent one leg, dug in a heel, twisted and flopped over on his back. Pain!

The two shapes came at him, blacking the sky, as Logan screamed at his fingers and the Gun fired and a ripper sliced in a smoking scorch across the black bodies and the two birds exploded and rained down in a bronze wreckage.

The brook was silver and cool softness over round rocks. On the shadowed moss bank, Jess dipped a cloth into the stream and carefully blotted the mangled flesh of Logan's back. He slept fitfully. Jess put aside the cloth and sat regarding him. She reached down to touch at his matted hair. His lips moved; he moaned. 'Jess . . . ' He tried to sit up, but she restrained him with gentle fingers.

'Lie still,' she told him. She could see the raw hurt in the wax of his skin, the fever of his eyes. For a moment he looked at her without recognition.

'Rest,' she said soothingly. 'You need rest.'

The tension began to leave him as he listened to her voice. Above him the tree boughs moved soft fans of shifting green shadow. The quiet worked on him as the last of the tension drained away. His breath evened. The pulse in his neck slowed and steadied.

'Got to keep moving,' he said. 'Ballard. Got to – '

'Hush,' she told him.

Now they were moving again, with Crazy Horse towering above them, impossibly huge. The warrior's feather was lost in cloud.

They had found the old trail, overgrown with years, leading into the base of the mountain. At its end was the main cavern entrance. Logan and Jess stepped into arched darkness. Their eyes gradually adjusted to the light change.

The floor was layered thickly with rock dust, undisturbed by footprints. Their feet echoed as they descended.

'Are you all right?' asked Jess.

'I can make it.'

The tunnel widened. They rounded an abrupt elbow turn and stopped.

The Thinker lay before them.

Here was a constellation of winking fireflies stretching to infinity. Here was an immense electronic silence. In the endless, glowing dark was Tangier and London, Macao and Capri and Beirut, El Quederef and Chateau-Chinon and Wounded Knee. From these caverns leapt the motive force of a dispensary in Chemnitz, a glasshouse in Shropshire, a callbox in Billings, Montana. . . . This vast mountain brain sent its signals along Earth's nervous system to the distant places, the villages, towns and cities, bringing order out of disorder, calmness out of confusion.

They beheld the world.

The final realization of the computer age. A direct extension of the electronic brains at Columbia and Cal Tech in the 1960s, it was a massive breakthrough in solid-state technology. Computer was linked with computer in ever widening complexity.

President Curtain was the first to suggest that the Thinker be moved from Niagara to the Crazy Horse Caverns, and with the death of the Republican Party in 1988 the Crazy Horse bill was passed without opposition. Estimated final cost: twenty-five billion dollars.

The old had built it; the young would use it.

'It's almost . . . *frightening*,' said Jess.

They moved downward along the spiral of tunnel. Spaced at irregular intervals along the glowing plain below were bars of darkness. Logan was perplexed. What did these dark areas represent? He would find out.

They stepped onto the polished flooring beside the first dark area. Set into the smooth computer metal facing them was an embossed plaque.

CATHEDRAL—JCV 6* 49883
West Complex. Los Angeles, California
Western America

A siren wail stabbed the silence. From deep within the hive of linking corridors something was coming in a sulfurous rush.

Logan snatched Jessica's hand and ran.

The sound intensified.

The thing was closing. It came with a howl and a shriek.

It was upon them.

They plunged into tunnel blackness. The siren ceased abruptly.

Tableau: Logan, braced against dead metal, the Gun a pointing finger; Jess, crouched behind him; and a looming presence at the mouth of the passage.

In the solenoid night the Watchman waited, motionless except for the faint gear-flicker behind the glass plate which was its face. A half-ton of destruction; armor plate bristling with weaponry. Waiting.

Doomed, thought Logan. Against this thing even a DS Gun was useless. What's holding him back? Why doesn't he go for us? Logan's throat moved. He looked up. Another plaque.

MULTI-OPERATIONAL LOWER LIFE UNIT—VJK
8* 1704
Pacific Ocean

Western Hemisphere

'M.O.L.L.U.,' breathed Logan. 'Molly!'

Of course, *that* was why the thing didn't attack them. That was why it couldn't move. This was a dead area. For the robot it didn't exist. Logan's thoughts raced. Cathedral. Molly. Both dead, untended stages on the Sanctuary line. Which meant the *next* dead area would be stage three. But how to get to it?

Logan backed Jess along the corridor. The Watchman didn't move. At the other end they faced brightness. The machine could not follow them down the dead passage; it would be forced to go around. But would they have enough time?

'Come on!' urged Logan.

They ran.

The Watchman burned into blinding motion.

They ran as the fox runs from the hounds. The darkness of another dead area was ahead. The Watchman erupted into the corridor, cannoned down upon them.

Into darkness!

The Watchman dead-stopped outside the tunnel.

Stage three:

WASHINGTON—LLI *7 5644
District of Columbia
Eastern America

'That's where the car out of Molly *should* have taken us,' said Logan. 'Ballard must be there, in Washington.'

'But how can we – That thing won't let us out,' said Jess.

Logan swept the area. 'I think there's another way,' he said.

Winding and zigzagging dizzily up above the mammoth electronic glow, a narrow series of steps had been chiseled into the tough interior rock of the mountain. To reach the steps, however, they would have to cover a full quarter-mile of live corridors.

Logan jammed the Gun into his belt and removed his shoes. He checked the Watchman. No movement. A silence.

Sucking in a lungful of air, Logan drew back his arm and lobbed one of the shoes far out across the top of the computer plain.

The shoe fell.

As it touched the metal floor the Watchman whirled and shrieked off down the hive.

'Go!'

The girl was terrified. 'We'll never make it. We'll – '

'Run, damn you, *run!*'

They sprinted for the steps.

The Watchman reached Logan's shoe, hummed for a split second; a muzzle glided in the robot's chest. It blitzed the shoe into flaked ash. The machine then reversed course, crashing back toward Logan and Jess.

The girl slipped to her knees on the polished floor. Logan pulled her up. They ran.

The Watchman's siren filled the world.

Running.

The glitter and flash of insect corridors.

Logan heaved the other shoe. It angled out and down, buying them another few seconds.

Running. The Watchman blurring in.

The steps!

Logan and Jess threw themselves onto the cut granite and scrambled upward – just as the Watchman slammed to a halt at the bottom.

'Will it follow us?'

'Can't,' Logan said, climbing. 'The steps aren't energized.'

'Where are we going?'

'Where they take us. Up.'

They kept climbing.

Steps and steps and steps.

Logan's wounded back throbbed; his jaw was a dull ache. Exhaustion dragged at him. The fitful rest on the bank had done little to strengthen him.

It grew darker as they ascended: the computer glow fading into gray shading into pitch. Logan was grateful for the darkness; he didn't want to see the steps falling steeply away below. Even the great plain of the Thinker far beneath him induced a sense of swimming vertigo. He would not look down again; he would look up. Up.

Logan froze, pulling Jess in beside him.

Someone was coming *down* the steps.

Was it Ballard?

Logan crouched close to the rock wall, eyes on the beam of light bobbing slowly toward them. The figure moved steadily down the twisting rope of steps. Now he was distinct enough for Logan to identify the tunic of a DS man. And the face. Not Ballard.

Francis.

Logan raised the Gun. Keeping his eyes tight on the advancing figure, he whispered, 'All right, Jess. It's up to you. You hate killing. He's a DS man, armed with a homer. Either I use my Gun first or he uses his. Which will it be?'

Silence.

'Jess . . . Jess?' Logan pivoted. The steps were empty.

Jess had vanished.

But how? He was stunned. Had she gone on back to – to where? Surely not to the thing which still waited for them at the bottom?

A soft voice called to him. 'Logan . . . here!'

He slid quick fingers along the rock. An opening.

Francis was twenty steps closer; his light flickered the walls.

Logan put away the Gun and slipped into the fissure, groping for Jess.

'Here. . . .'

He touched her ankle.

'Go on ahead,' he urged. 'I'll follow you.'

The crawl-space narrowed. Narrowed more. They were flesh corks in a pipe. A muffled sob. Jess could go no further. The weight of Crazy Horse pressed around them. Logan felt the rush of claustrophobia, shut it off.

'I think it's a little wider ahead,' whispered Jess.

'Stretch,' he told her, speaking harshly. 'We can't go back.'

Her hips scraped against the rough, sinuous pipe; she inched ahead.

Now they could move on hands and knees. The ceiling had risen. They stood upright in the blind core of the great mountain.

The rough talus of the stone floor cut into Logan's bare feet. The dark was impenetrable.

'Which way?' asked Jess.

Logan took her hand and began a cautious advance. With a bare foot he encountered emptiness, caught his balance, drew back. 'Not this way.' He tried another direction. The floor was pocked with deep shafts; a moment's carelessness and they would fall. The murmur of subterranean waters echoed up to them.

Logan probed ahead, weaving between the sinkholes in the stone. On all sides, in the living blackness, his ears could detect the shift of distances and depths.

A smooth rock face. Logan cautiously felt his way along it, searching for an opening. The rock face curved. They were in a closed chamber. Abruptly his hands fingered emptiness: the climb and twist of a passage. They heard the slow drip of water. Where did it lead?

They'd lost the sense of sight and now all sense of direction.

'Keep going,' he said.

They clambered up flowstone ridges, snaked between stalactites and stalagmites and wet limestone columns. They were in a black mole-land of dolomite and calcite and gypsum. The mineral breath of the caverns blew on them.

Jess suddenly collapsed. Logan knelt, held her against him. 'Rest a moment,' he told her.

Now, with the cessation of their movement, they heard

other sounds in the pitch. Something plopped into a pool. Hard claws clicked on stone. A rustling insect scuttled over Jessica's leg. She screamed, surged to her feet, shuddering, as a second and a third claw-footed creature crawled her flesh. Whipping at her skin, she frantically dislodged them.

'Wait,' said Logan. 'I think I can give us some light.'

He twisted the pearl endplate of the gun, lifted the plate free. The glow from the Gun's interior power pack dimly illuminated the space around them.

The chamber was acrawl with cavernicolous life: in the shallow pools lived crayfish and salamanders, whose optic ganglia had atrophied. These blind fish had developed tactile papillae on their heads, arranged in ridges. The lava walls supported Harvestmen spiders spinning gray clockcurl webs. Adelops swarmed the floors, preying on mites and myriapods among the dark mold and fungi. Here they had lived and adapted since the Permian and Cretaceous periods. And here, too, were the beetles and wingless insects. By the thousands.

Logan and Jess fled the chamber.

They hurried onward, along deep-winding cuts and narrow cracks in the substrata. Jess stopped at the edge of a wide pool of black water. She was breathing in ragged gasps, her body shaking with exhaustion. 'I – I can't go – on.'

'If we stay here we die.'

'We'll die anyway. We're hopelessly lost. Admit it.'

'All right, we're lost.'

'And the caverns go on forever. We'll die here. We'll fall and be crushed or starve....'

Logan studied the water revealed by the Gun's glow. A wet flash. 'We won't starve,' he said grimly.

He was soaked to the armpits when he brought up the darting silver fish. It wriggled in his fist. Logan climbed back to the girl and the Gun that lay beside her.

'We won't starve,' he said again. 'In fact, if we –' He paused, staring.

'What is it?'

Logan triumphantly thrust the creature toward her. 'This fish. It's not like all the others. This fish has *eyes*!'

He quickly reassembled the Gun.

'Let's go,' he said. 'Into the water.'

Up the coursing stream that fed the pool, ducking their heads to avoid the rock ceiling that lowered and raised above them. Around two sharp bends. Swimming. Climbing as they swam.

'Look!'

Sunshine ahead.

They climbed faster as light filled the cave.

They came out beneath a clean, cold waterfall that speared white music into a deep gorge.

They breathed the bright, clear air.

5

He glides the cave darkness, guided by the glow-flicker of the Follower.

His quarry is ahead, but it is not wise to attempt a chase in these caverns.

He retraces his path, leaves the tunnels and climbs uncounted steps into the head of Crazy Horse.

He peers through the right eye of the great warrior, sees Logan and the girl. They are far away, moving through the scrub toward the high grass.

He smiles.

He has them now.

There is nowhere for them to go.

EARLY AFTERNOON . . .

'LET'S PIDGE!' CRIED GRAYGIRL.

Deesticker jay.
Lift me a day.
Wanna' me forever
On a PeeGee way.

A skirl of lung music, recorder and flageolet.

Deesticker jay,
Wild me away.
Me gotta never
Kinda stickerlift play!

The pleasure gypsies came in jeweled laughter. They fireballed the Black Hills. Their devilsticks flamed.

Deesticker,
Deesticker,
AAAAAAAaaaaaaaaaaa . . .

Logan heard the shrill piping as he and Jess cleared the high grass. 'Down!' He gestured her back, out of sight.

In a glitter and swoop the gypsies were upon him.

'Footfella, hey!'

A blast of volcano heat behind Logan. The devilstick chopped the Gun from his hand as it passed. Another struck him at chest level.

He was down, ringed in a circle of jato fire.

'If Sandfella tickles, giva he a fry!'

Logan did not move. He knew of the gypsies. Their first leader had been a full-blooded Apache named Jimmy Walks-Like-a-Wolf who went berserk in the aftermath of the Little War. Gathering a crew of psychotics about him, he had conceived the gypsy death pact, the ritual vow of self-destruction. No pleasure gypsy lived long enough to see his flower go black; each was sworn to die on red as a gesture of ultimate defiance against the system. They feared neither Sleep nor Sandman. They were a law unto themselves.

A sword-slim man in white dismounted from a stick, and walked from the low-hovering vehicle to Logan. 'Sandfella up,' he said.

Logan stood up. He faced Rutago, king of the devilsticks. Sixteen. Bearded. White silks. Flat-muscled. Golden curls. A beauty. He reached over, turned up Logan's right hand. 'Blinker he,' said Rutago. He gave the others his smile.

Graygirl joined her man. She regarded Logan with lynx eyes. 'Givva he Sandfella Lastday *wild*!'

The pleasure gypsies were fourteen in number. Seven men, seven women. Youngest: fifteen. Oldest: seventeen.

The females were satins and brocades and goldwire mesh. They were glittermake and richly coiffed hair, star-piled; their nails opalescent and striped with lapis lazuli metallics. They were scented and soaped and smelled of peaches. (Graygirl was the exception. She wore no makeup; only her eyes were striped in black. She was starkly beautiful.)

The males were skinsilks and kidleather fringe and cuffed velvet boots. They were filigreed in silverstitch and platinum. They were brushed and oiled and immaculate.

Two of the pleasure girls came forward, holding Jessica between them. 'Gotta more than sandfella,' said one. 'Gotta we a runnergirl.'

Logan took a step toward Jess, but the jato fire still hemmed him. He looked sourly at the circle of devilsticks, their jet-flamed pods ready to sear him if he made an improper move.

These were not the devilsticks he'd ridden as a boy; these were fast and deadly, and the thrust from their rear-mounted chromaly jato housings could char a man down in the snap of a finger. If I could break this circle maybe I could handle them, thought Logan. Just *maybe*.

Rutago seemed pleased with the situation. He waved a graceful, jewel-encrusted hand. 'Tie fella, runnergirl. Takeum on a stickerlift.'

Three of the male gypsies stepped into the circle to bind Logan's wrists with tapewire.

They led him to Rutago's machine. The devilstick gleamed richly, from its hand-scrolled leather saddle studded with diamonds, emeralds, sapphires and fire rubies, to the inlay of pearls set into the long stick-body of the swift pleasure craft.

Logan settled himself behind the stitched saddle, and his legs were tapewired under him. Jess was similarly mounted and tied on Graygirl's stick.

'Deestickers go!'

The pleasure gypsies jetted.

Logan's Gun lay in the grass, abandoned.

The fiery wheel of the noon sun blistered its slow way across the Dakota sky, crowding the thin dry air with waves of shimmering heat. Deadwood was dust and ghost town stillness. The squat, wind-worked buildings along the main street had long since been scoured of paint, and their weathered boards reared up crookedly from the red earth.

A man lounged back into the porch shadow of the Big Dog Saloon, boots propped lazily on the spur-scarred rail. His lizard-lidded eyes raised to a distant shout: 'Stickereeeeeeeeee.' The man stood up, peered down the dust-hazed street.

The gypsy riders passed the lookout posted at the edge of Deadwood and arrived at the Big Dog in a bright, chattering cluster.

They dismounted, led their prisoners inside.

The saloon was lavishly furnished. Velvet couches. Ivory chairs. Green baize tables. Ornate lamps of shell pearl. Tapestries and bead hangings. The long mahogany bar was polished to a high gloss. Behind the bar hung a garish oil painting of a coyly smiling nude.

Logan and Jess were herded into the room, wrists still secured.

Rutago made his entrance, a heavy saddlebag across one silked shoulder. He dropped the bag carelessly at his feet. From it spilled gypsy riches taken on the raid: sprays, pendants, seed pearls, ribbons of garnet and topaz and amethyst. In the heaped mound were cabochon stones, onyx and agate. With a connoisseur's care, Rutago plucked out one tiny pigeon-blood ruby. He breathed on it, rubbed it along his silk thigh until static electricity crackled from the faceted surface. 'Like me a rubyrock. Took it from a merchantman,' he said.

Rutago walked forward to stand in front of Logan. He

slowly unscrewed the jewel face from a Borgia ring and held it to Logan's nose. Logan sniffed cautiously and choked.

Hemodrone! The bitter smell of the ritual gypsy poison lingered in his nostrils. One swallow and a man would begin to die. Unless the victim received an antidote he would continue to die slowly as the hemoglobin of his blood absorbed the virulent poison. It would take hours and bring great pain. Logan instinctively clamped his teeth together.

Rutago smiled, blinked sleepily, turned away. He crossed to Jess. Two of the females gripped her elbows as Rutago deftly pried open her lips and poured the Hemodrone down her throat. She coughed and strangled.

Logan thrust himself at Rutago, but was driven to his knees by a numbing blow.

'Sandfella must behave or runnergirl die,' said Rutago. 'Gotta earn the antidote.'

One of the females approached Logan with a first-aid kit. 'Sandfella turnabout,' she ordered. He obeyed.

The girl severed the tapewire binding his wrists. Then she gentled away his torn shirt, exposing the crusted wounds along his back. She adjusted the kit, placed it at the top of one of the deep cuts and drew it slowly downward. A trail of fresh pink synthaskin formed behind it as the wound healed. She tended his other cuts and abrasions, while a second female treated Jess.

Logan was given a clean white shirt and boots for his bruised feet.

The antidote. Logan knew he could not take Jess away without it. Even if they broke free he couldn't take her to a populated area, where the antidote might be found, because of her palm flower. As a runner she'd be doomed. But did they really have the antidote here? The gypsy might be lying. Yet he'd have to trust them. He had no other choice.

'How do I earn the antidote?' Logan asked Rutago.

The gypsy smiled, nodded toward the pleasure girls. They crowded close to Logan. Blue eyes, brown eyes, hazel eyes, green eyes, golden eyes, gray eyes, radiated heat.

'And what happens to Jess?'

Rutago scooped the jewelry back into the saddlebag. He

then regally offered Jessica his hand and escorted her up the stairs.

One of the males said sweetly, 'Rutago he a Ribbonrider, but also he a loverman. After he, the rest of we. Runnergirl a lucky one.'

The seven pleasure girls guided Logan out of the main room, along a hallway, into a chamber at the rear of the saloon, a boudoir, dominated by an Emperor bed over which was spread a pale snow coverlet of imported satin.

Led by Graygirl, the females removed Logan's clothing. They led him to the cleansing room, adjusted the temperature to blood heat, and pushed him under the needle suds. He was dried by warm air currents, scented and powdered. Then he was given an injection of Everlove.

In the boudoir the girls awaited him. They were all goldenly nude and reclined at the foot of the bed on which lay Graygirl. She was somber and colorless and lovely. She took Logan's hand as he walked over to her, gazed up into his eyes, and smiled a sleek cat's smile. 'Wild me, Sandfella,' she said to him in a husky voice. She ran her fingers along his thigh. 'Bedabye me.'

And the others smiled with her. The green-eyed female said, 'Wild she, Sandlover. Then wild we!'

The first orgasm was good.

The second orgasm was all right.

The third orgasm was bad.

The fourth orgasm was painful.

The fifth orgasm was agony.

The sixth orgasm was damnation.

And where was Jess, and what were they doing to her? And where was the antidote?

In the upstairs room Rutago lay waiting. The floor was spread with his jewels and glittered: a lake of gemfire. The cleansing room door opened.

Rutago nodded. 'Come you runnergirl me.'

Jessica moved toward him over the jeweled floor, her face emotionless. She wore a flowrobe of silver mesh.

The gypsy peeled away her robe, pulled Jess down upon him.

She was wood.

He stroked and petted her.

She was wood.

He kissed her deeply, fondled her with desperate hands.

She was wood.

Jessica stood at the long bar while Rutago paced. His face was flushed and angry.

'Keep your promise,' said Logan. 'Give her the – '

'Antidote, *no*!'

Logan tensed his fists. 'We both did what you wanted.'

Rutago smiled savagely at Jess. 'Cheated by a runnergirl. Didn't try hard enough. Now we use another lift.'

'Pull a tooth of runnergirl,' said one of the males brightly. 'Maybe pull a fingernail.'

'Gotta me another lift,' said Rutago, waving aside the suggestion. He eyed Logan jealously. 'Sandfella's gonna do it.'

Logan read the effect of the poison in Jess. Her face was ashen, her breathing shallow. The Hemodrone was running her blood. And, for the moment, there was nothing he could do. Nothing.

Four of the gypsies lifted Jess onto the polished bartop. They held her wrists and ankles. The others waited expectantly. The play was Rutago's.

The gypsy leader savored his power; he advanced and placed his hands on Logan's shoulders in comradely fashion. 'Runnergirl she soon a sick one. Wanta you the antidote?'

Logan nodded tightly.

'Then' – Rutago handed a short bone-handled dirk to Logan – 'gotta take an ounce of flesh – anywhere on runnergirl.'

Logan paled. No, he couldn't do this. The act was inhuman. *And was a homer human?* They were asking him to torture the girl who'd saved his life.

But she'd die if he didn't.

'Anywhere?'

Rutago nodded. His smile was angelic.

Graygirl placed a delicate set of spring balance scales on the bar. One tiny pan held a gold ounce.

Logan bent over Jess. She had her eyes closed, which was fortunate, because if she watched him . . . He slit the clothing along her hip to expose a patch of white skin. He placed his hand high on her upper leg. Shielded by his body, his thumb searched for the nerve plexus on her inner thigh. Shifting his weight to cover the action, he dug his thumb powerfully into the pressure point. Jess winced.

Then he used the knife. Quickly. Efficiently.

The raw square of bleeding flesh balanced the scales. Logan tossed the dirk aside.

Rutago looked steadily at him. He shook his head slowly. 'Sandfella badfella. Badfella cheat. Antidote, no.'

Enough!

Logan swept an arm around Graygirl, dropped to one knee and bowed the girl across it. 'Give her the antidote, or I break this bitch's back!'

Graygirl was no longer gray; she was red-faced with pain, her eyes bulging, her mouth twisted.

Rutago stood unmoving, undecided.

'*Now!*' snapped Logan. His hands tightened.

'Third finger, left hand,' rasped Graygirl.

Disgusted, Rutago extended the ring facing. Logan sniffed it, was satisfied.

Rutago poured the contents into a glass of water, handed it to Jess. Trembling, sweat sparkling her skin, she gulped it down.

Logan motioned her out. 'Take a stick and ride for the Gun,' he told her. 'I'll catch up with you.'

Jess limped to the door, moved through it.

A thrum of metal. She was gone.

Logan waited to give Jess a proper start, then backed out slowly, holding Graygirl in front of him. With vicious force, he heaved her back through the batwing door into the midst of the gypsies, spilling them.

Outside, he vaulted into the saddle of the nearest devilstick and kicked the release stud. The hovercraft flamed into motion.

He knew they'd be after him. Trees whiplashed at him as he skimmed their top branches. He'd stay as close to the ground as possible, head into the brush country and try to shake the pursuit before doubling back for Jess.

As a boy, Logan had loved devilsticks. But this brute took some getting used to. Its power thrust was massive and tricky, and a delicate touch was needed to keep upright. Sudden throttle bursts were dangerous, threatening to pitch him from the saddle. Yet his confidence grew with each passing mile. Learning to *feel* the machine he rode, beginning to understand its quickworking habits, Logan felt real exhilaration as he jetted over the country. His wounds were healed and his hands were free.

Let the gypsies come!

Logan saw them as he topped a high rock rise. Six of them, expertly riding his wake. He cut his vehicle sharply down into a baked creek bed, hugging ground, his jet flame searing the dry dust.

He had taken Graygirl's stick, and it was fast. Faster, by far, than most of the others. Gradually they fell back. And back. And were lost behind him.

Logan headed for Jess.

Yet one rider clung to him, matching his speed, gaining with each twist and fold of land. The afternoon sun rayed on moving jewels.

Rutago.

Logan gave his craft full throttle, but the gypsy continued to gain, mile by mile.

At the entrance to the Lame Johnny, Logan spotted Jess. She was just over a mile ahead, riding in a ragged, irregular pattern, weak from loss of blood and unable to control her vehicle properly. Sheer guts had carried her this far; she could falter at any moment.

Logan sped to catch her.

Rutago charged closer, giving the wind his smile.

The Lame Johnny was below, and Logan bounced in the saddle as the swift currents affected his power thrust. He cut to the right, using the bank, and his speed resumed. Rutago was almost upon him.

The king was here, the man who rode the Ribbon. Logan had heard of this legendary feat. Many deestickers had tried it, tried to hug that flexible durasteel cable stretching the storm-tossed Atlantic, but only one jockey had ever ridden the Ribbon from shore to shore, through wind and wave change, cold and blind fog. Only Rutago had managed it. The king.

Logan braced himself for attack. And was shocked.

In a wash of jato heat Rutago sliced past him, heading for Jess.

The gypsy raked the side of her jato housing. She wavered as smoke began seeping from her craft. It staggered downward, the girl fighting for control. Rutago circled, lazily riding air, expertly guiding his machine, playing her.

Jess regained partial stability, and he was at her again immediately, forcing her close to the red granite walls of the ravine. Her face held terror; in another moment she'd be spilled from the saddle.

Logan shot up to engage the gypsy, flashed by him, drawing him away from Jess in a hazardous ploy: Logan took his stick up the sheer ravine face, riding the mountain with the water boiling below them.

Rutago could not resist the bait. He made splendid use of his fabled skill to harass Logan, dipping and slashing in at him. Logan was a boy once again, all awkwardness and uncertainty in trying to handle his first devilstick. This man who knifed at him was in cool command of the air, but when would he tire of the one-sided game.

He'll go for Jess again unless . . . *unless I kill him*. But how?

Logan kicked his craft around, aimed it at the gypsy. Rutago veered left; Logan veered with him, fixing his trajectory. Full throttle. A startled look on Rutago's face as Logan pitched himself from the saddle.

Down . . . down . . . down. The Lame Johnny far below. Rapids. White water. Logan arrowed toward it in a long dive.

The stick caught Rutago below the rib line, carrying away his stomach as it drove into the face of the ravine.

Logan sliced the water, and the rapids took him, rolled him twisting, sucked him under. He came up choking, kicking to maintain leverage. Rocks just ahead.

The last thing Logan saw before he went under again was the faltering smoke trail of Jessica's wounded machine layering the sky.

4

He knows the girl is on black now. A runner.

But the quarry has vanished again beyond Crazy Horse.

He checks the board in Rapid City. It does not help him. The Follower remains dark.

He is certain that Logan and the girl must break cover soon.

When they do he will be ready.

He will be there to intercept them.

AFTERNOON . . .

JESS LAY UNCONSCIOUS in a pale square of sunlight next to her damaged machine. One cheek was scraped raw where she had skidded along the black asphalt. The wound on her thigh still pulsed blood.

She didn't hear the soft footsteps or the voices that surrounded her. Fourteen bright eyes peered down.

'Ohhhhhhhh!'

'Pret-ty, pret-ty!'

Seven tiny moppets in pink playrompers drew back in alarm as the girl stirred. Jess moaned, lapsed back into unconsciousness. The children bent over the still figure. Wonderingly, they felt her hair, her soft lips, the long lashes of her closed eyes.

'What is it?'

'It's a people! Ohhh . . . so *big*!'

'People tired.'

They clucked together, deciding that Jess should be in a crib. They tugged and lifted and pulled her toward the Cribroom.

Fourteen bright eyes peered down. Jess lay on her side in a small crib, knees tucked under her chin. The crib had sensed her hurt and ministered to her, closing her wounds with synthaskin. She slept deeply.

The eyes never left her.

DAKOTA STATES
INDUSTRIAL NURSERY—UNIT K

Beneath the sign Logan reconnoitered the gray metalmesh fence. Twice as tall as a man and capped with a triple strand of microwire. These gossamer threads could chop off fingers under the weight of a climber.

Beyond the fence, far out on the flat surface of the nursery playground, he could see the wreckage of Jessica's devilstick. Apparently she was inside somewhere, perhaps already in the hands of the Autogoverness. Other runners had tried to hide in these vast institutions, but each Autogoverness was programed to sound an alarm. And if you *could* avoid the robots there were always the older children, conditioned and hypnotaped against invaders.

But I've got to try and find her.

He had to walk a full mile along the fence perimeter before he found the tree. It angled up and inward; one of its branches thrust out toward the wire. Logan climbed the tree, inching out as far along the branch as he dared. He hung there. Six feet ahead of him, and down, were the deadly strands of microwire.

He began to swing himself back and forth, gathering momentum. If he struck the wires they'd slice him like cheese. At the height of a swing he let go, twisting his body in the air. Logan hit ground safely, rolled and came up in a crouch. Silence. No alarms.

He crossed the wide asphalt toward the looming bulk of the nursery. At its fortress flank he paused to orient himself. He'd grown up in a place like this. The hypno classes would be in the west wing, the dorms to the left. He was now outside the infant wards. Less chance of being discovered if he entered here. High up the brick building face was a bank of windows. Logan began to climb, clinging to the irregular surface. A foot slipped; he regained his balance and continued.

The first window was locked.

He spidered along a narrow ledge, feeling the strain pulling at his arm muscles. The next window was unlocked but jammed. He struggled to budge it; the glass panel grated inward. Logan crawled through, dropped to the floor and stood listening. He was in a storage area.

Where was Jess? She could be anywhere in the sprawl of buildings. She could be hurt and dying in a corridor or under a conveyor or hidden in a locker space. Or maybe she wasn't here at all. The silence encouraged him. If Jess *were* here, at least she hadn't been discovered as yet.

He crossed the room and eased open the door. Distantly he heard the hum and buzz of classrooms in use. He checked the hall. Deserted. He moved to the next door. The dot symbol told him it was a Playroom.

It was not activated. The vibroballs were boxed and motionless, no longer bouncing themselves in puzzle patterns from the walls. The talk puppets were stacked and speechless. The echo boards were silent. No sign of Jess here. He closed the door.

The next chamber was also quiet. The Deliveryroom. Logan checked the moveways. He stared in fascination at the Hourglass, at the phosphorescent crystals in the thick globe which gave each infant his birthright – the radioactive time-flower. He stared at his own hand, blinking red-black, red-black. . . . He'd received *his* crystal in a room like this; it had imbedded the flower in his right palm, and the crystal had decayed on schedule, in the same way the cesium atom decays in a radium clock, turning the stigmata inexorably from yellow to blue to red – and now, soon, to black.

Logan passed through the room to a long corridor. Had Jess gone in this direction? The search seemed hopeless, but he could not abandon it. Not until he was forced to.

A whirring noise – a sound Logan had heard often in his childhood. The Autogoverness.

He jerked open a door to his right, dodged inside. The door swung closed. The interior was dark and warm.

'My own, my precious,' his mother said.

A softness enveloped him.

'My little one, my sweet,' said the Loveroom. Its voice was a crooning, soothing music. 'There, there,' said the room.

Logan attempted to struggle, but the room held him fast in tender embrace, stroked him. It pressed him against its great warm bosom and rocked him gently, rhythmically. 'My dove, my darling, my precious love.'

'But – I can't – ' said Logan wildly.

His mother held him close.

'I can't stay here. I've got to – '

'Sleep,' said the room softly.

Need and emotional hunger flooded through Logan in a great wave.

'Mother loves you, loves you, loves you,' sang the room.

'No,' cried Logan, 'I've got to – '

'Sleep,' said the room.

'I've got to . . .'

'Sleep.' Insistently, lovingly.

'Got to . . . sleep,' sighed Logan.

He slept.

In Cribroom L-16, during her hourly inspection, Autogoverness K-110 discovered a sleeping woman.

The Autogoverness calmly rolled into the corridor and activated the Invader Alarm. Bells. Sirens.

Jess awoke in panic, leaped from the small crib and began to run.

The nursery defended its children. Doors slammed, gates closed; trams and moveways halted. Crib covers snapped down like turtle shells; barriers sprung up through slotted floors, sealing off each wing.

Invaders!

Repel!

Protect!

Defend!

The door of the Loveroom was wrenched open. Logan was there. 'Jess – this way!'

In the alarm din they fled along corridors crowded with curious children. An Autogoverness rolled at them, clucking; Logan disabled it with a savage heel blow. They slid under a descending barrier, whipped through a closing door, avoided a handler machine. They clattered down to the first floor as the building entrance was sliding shut along its lubricated tracks.

'Faster!' Logan yelled.

They cleared the massive slide-door a split second before it locked home. The edge of the door rapped Logan's shoulder, knocking him off stride – but they were out of the building.

They sprinted across the playground for the main gate.

It was closed.

Logan broke into the glass control booth, smashed the panel, and jerked down the release switch.

The gate swung open.

A roboguard tried to stop them, but Logan evaded it, grabbed Jessica by the arm and cut into a field. They disappeared down a weed-choked bar ditch that angled into the woods.

The Rapid City concourse was jammed with citizens when they arrived on the maze platform. Logan had retrieved his Gun, and it was safely out of sight against his ribs. Jess kept her right hand fisted to conceal her charflower. Still, Logan knew, the scanners would pick them up if they tried to board a mazecar.

'Stay back here, close to the wall,' he told Jess.

He sifted through the crowd. A ruddy-faced man bumped him. The man's arms were full of souvenirs from the western states; a triangular felt banner extending from his collar proclaimed *Cheyenne Frontier Days. LET 'ER BUCK!* Perched on the top of the heap of packages was a tiny outhouse carved from polished redwood. When the citizen bumped Logan the outhouse fell to the platform. Logan picked it up, put it back on the pile.

'Thanks, citizen! Ya-hoooo!'

'Ya-hooooo!' replied Logan, forcing a smile.

He reached the scanner box, opened it casually in the manner of a repairman. Reaching in, he shorted out the unit.

Returning to Jess, he hurried her toward the boarding slots. She stumbled, put out a hand to steady herself. In that brief gesture she revealed her black palmflower, and a woman on the edge of the crowd screamed, 'Runner!'

A ripple of movement; shouting voices, shock.

A man was about to enter a mazecar. Logan thrust him back and they leaped aboard.

The angry crowd dropped away behind them and was lost as the car burrowed into the long tunnel. The continent rushed under and over and around them.

Logan knew the dangers. Unless DS blundered – and DS never blundered – there would already be operatives at the Rapid City platform checking their departure. Within seconds DS would know exactly which car they were on, which tunnel they were in. Dispatchers would alert units all along the route.

The car suddenly faltered. Slowed. Slotted into a siding.

'They've stopped us,' said Logan. 'Out!'

'Where are we?' asked Jess.

'No questions. Hurry.'

As the hatch opened and they made their exit Logan caught a sub-lim flicker on the mazecar viewscreen.

It said what they always said: *Duty. Don't run!*

Union artillery batteries were destroying Fredericksburg when Logan and Jess reached ground level.

Snipers had fired on the Federal troops preparing to cross the Rappahannock River, and General Burnside had ordered his cannon to level the town. He would then occupy Fredericksburg and advance into the hills to clean out the Confederate stronghold. It was a foolhardy plan, this direct frontal assault on an impregnable position, and Burnside had been warned against it, but he'd refused to alter his decision. His battle plan would be carried out despite the odds. He was determined to wipe out the Rebels on their own ground and give the North a great victory.

Now the pontoon boats were being readied for the river crossing. Bluecoated officers on horseback were directing the operation. Ponderous wagons and heavy brass artillery pieces were being rolled on to the wooden boats.

Burnside studied the south shore through a pair of field-glasses. A church steeple tottered and fell under the barrage; a tall brick structure folded into rubble. Burnside lowered the glasses, rubbing at his long black whiskers. He looked about twenty. 'We'll give those Johnny Rebs a real whuppin' right enough!' he declared. 'They'll remember this day.'

The general's aide looked concerned. 'I hear Lee is on the slope with Longstreet. And Stonewall Jackson commands their right flank. It's going to be extremely difficult, sir.'

Burnside snorted. 'War is never easy, Major. You do what you must for your country.'

The aide saluted and returned to his men.

Ambrose E. Burnside was a robot, an android, built to the exact specifications of the famed Civil War officer. His mass of blue-clad androids would engage gray-clad androids for a day and a night in the Battle of Fredericksburg in a compressed re-creation of the bloody slaughter of 1862, when more than twelve thousand men died on these Virginia slopes. Field pieces would flash from hidden embrasures. Breakaway buildings would collapse on schedule. Cannon balls would strike into ranks of breakaway robots, who would lose arms and legs and heads in brutally realistic fashion. The snowpatched ground would be stained with crimson fluids.

Logan and Jess edged into the pack of excited tourists and Virginia citizenry crowding the view areas.

'Duty,' a loudspeaker blared above the din. 'That's what you'll see here today, citizens. Loyalty. Courage. The willingness to die for one's country in order to preserve it. The Civil War was fought by seventeen- and eighteen-year-olds, men willing to die for their cause. They did not question their duty or flinch from the face of death. They sacrificed themselves willingly, gloriously. Now – watch them charge, citizens, in this heroic battle, shown to you as it happened 254 years ago. And remember, there were no runners at Fredericksburg!'

Jess looked at the terrain facing them. Artificially created fog cloaked the ground. Cannon added a bass rumble to the sharp snap of musketry. The ground rose up in gouts as shot and ball plowed it.

Silently Logan guided Jess toward the river. A deep drainage ditch led to the tents of Burnside's camp, and they began to crawl along this, away from the view area.

The ditch angled around to the rear of the encampment. Logan knew they didn't have to worry about any of the androids giving out an alarm. Each robot soldier was programed to play its assigned part in the battle.

They clambered up the drainage bank and ducked under the canvas flap of a Union tent. Two perfectly formed androids were standing motionless inside, ready to step from the tent when their circuits commanded them. Their blank sixteen-year-old faces were frozen.

Logan struck them to the ground and began to strip off their clothing. 'Put this on,' he said, tossing Jess a Federal uniform.

Logan buttoned the blue tunic, stuffing the Gun into it. He looped a canteen around his shoulder, picked up a long musket. Jess also took a musket. In the soiled uniform, with a Union cap pulled over her hair, she could pass as a soldier so long as they stayed well back from the view areas.

'Now stick close to me,' he said, 'and do what I do.'

A bugle sounded the call to arms.

Logan and Jess joined the Grand Army of the Potomac. They climbed into one of the slab-sided boats, sharing the craft with a dozen other Bluecoats during its passage across the shallow river.

They scrambled up the mud bank into Fredericksburg and moved cautiously through the gutted town. Broken-backed buildings smoked in ruin. The crackle of musketry filled the air. Metal bees hummed. Hill cannon belched bronze thunder. As they walked, the churned mud of the street sucked at their boots.

More bugles. The rattle of drums. Burnside was preparing his assault. On the far right, blue ranks were faltering under the guns of Stonewall Jackson.

They faced Marye's Heights, rising up in a steepening incline from a wide plain spattered with artificial snow. The Heights were manned by the crack Washington Artillery of New Orleans, pride of the South. Robert E. Lee was up there with the Grays, giving them his strength, and the entrenched Confederates has mounted some 250 field pieces to rake the slopes below.

To the left the holiday concourse was jammed with spectators: bright tunics, flags and the ocean roar of happy people. A darkness there. A *black* tunic! DS! Francis! Had he seen them, guessed at their destination? Was he, even now, raising his Gun to homer them? Logan turned back to the hill, pulled his cap lower.

The girl's face was gray. She looked at Logan helplessly. He pointed off to the right. 'We have to get across the battlefield, to the other side.'

'They'll see us.'

'Not if we move up the slope with Burnside's men. Once past the wall over Marye's Heights we'll be all right. There's a maze tunnel I used to play in as a boy. They don't use it much since they built New Fredericksburg and reconverted the area.'

'C'mon, lads!' yelled an android officer near Logan. 'Let's show the Rebs our steel!'

In a wash of fife and drum and bugle and bright regimental flags, the boys in blue marched out into columns-of-four, muskets forward, a tide of bayonets moving up.

'Keep your head lowered,' he told Jess. 'And stay out of the depressions. That's where the cannons are programed to hit.'

They were a third of the way up, in ordered rank, and the hill guns were quiet. Getting the range. Letting the sheep march close enough to slaughter. 'Burnside's blunder' they called it for two centuries after. Burnside, the fool, the pompous clown with his mutton-chop whiskers, sending his troops to certain death in a vain bid for personal glory. Little wonder that Lincoln replaced him after Fredericksburg.

A pulsing silence.

The cannons emptied their iron throats.

Inferno!

Jess pressed close to Logan, inching up the snowed slope as the withering storm of canister exploded around them. Androids screamed, dropped muskets, pitched forward. Robot horses pawed air, gushed crimson. Bugles ceased in midcry.

Marye's Hill was a tumult of shrieking metal death.

'Don't falter now, lads!' cried a hatless lieutenant behind them. 'Forward – for Lincoln and the Union! Hurrah, hurrah!'

A cannon ball cut him in half.

Just ahead of them, concealed behind a stretch of uneven stone wall fronting Sunken Road, a contingent of sharpshooting Georgians and North Carolinians rose up to pour a hot hail of musket fire into the still-advancing Federals.

The lines were falling back.

As Logan reached the base of the wall at Sunken Road a musket shot dropped him to his knees. He was momentarily breathless, but alive; the canteen across his chest had absorbed the ball.

Artillery crashed through oak woods. Fleeced smoke from

hill cannon lazed the sky, mingling with the curtain of ground fog.

Where was Jess? Logan scanned the slope for sign of her.

Near him, a gray-clad figure was shaking a fist and shouting in mock triumph, 'Skeedaddle, you Bluebellies! Back to yer holes. *EEEEeeee-yow!*'

Several Confederates had fallen behind the wall, but other robots had filled in along the barrier. Logan was ignored as he stripped off his uniform, discarding it along with his musket.

The gallop of an advancing horse. A stern-faced man on a white stallion, saber in hand. Bearded, uniformed in splendor. 'Fine, boys, fine,' boomed Robert E. Lee. 'There'll be extra rations for all when this day's done.' His voice was considerably amplified in order to reach the crowd in the view areas. He galloped back down the line.

The attack has been completely broken now, and the Blues were in full rout.

Then, clearly, Logan saw Jess – far down the slope. The girl was struggling against a tide of moving androids. Caught up in the knot of retreating figures, she was swept back down the long hill toward the viewing stands.

Back toward Francis.

3

He knows they are both in his grasp.
The crowds block him, frustrate him.
His anticipation is mounting.
He savors this, as the hunting cat savors the kill.
Close.
Very close.

LATE AFTERNOON . . .

FACES. THOUSANDS OF FACES. But none of them Jessica's.

Logan was jostled and pushed in the holiday mansprawl along the concourse. Tourist laughter, shouts.

'Hey, citizen.'

Logan looked down at an eight-year-old. Redhead, with freckles and serious blue eyes. The boy was selling souvenirs. He held up a small brass cannon. 'Fires a real ball, citizen. Put an eye out with it, if you've a mind to try. Genuine treasured memento of the Annual Civil War Gala, imported from Monte Carlo.'

'No . . . no, I don't want one.'

The boy did not argue; he dipped away into the mob flow.

Logan paused at a doorway, letting the throng eddy past. He drew back. A black tunic, coming toward him. Francis!

Logan pressed into the doorway. It proved to be the entrance to a Re-Live parlor. He craned his neck to see over the bobbing heads of the crowd. The black figure was still advancing, appearing and disappearing in the press. Closer with each step.

A robot touched his arm. 'Citizen Wentworth 10,' said the robot, looking with steel sympathy at Logan's blinking hand. 'We've been expecting you. This way, please.'

He had no choice. Francis was outside, back to the door, studying the crowd.

The robot slid out a life drawer from the metal wall.

'Just lie down here. This is our latest model. You may switch years as desired.'

Logan settled into the steel foam seat, grateful to be shielded from the open doorway. The robot dabbed his temples with saline solution, connected the rubber-cradled terminals to his neck and forehead.

'Listen, I don't really need to be . . .' Logan was stalling for time, but the robot was programed to deal smoothly with nervous citizens on Lastday.

'Any year – as desired,' he repeated, flipping a switch. The life drawer slid silently into the wall.

Darkness.

I can't stay here. I have to find Jess. I –

He was sixteen, and the Nevada desert was a brown heat shimmer before his eyes. Logan sat in the sparse shade of a saguaro cactus, utterly motionless except for his eyes. One hundred miles of desert to cover without food, water or weapons to graduate from DS school. Now, in the second day, he was dehydrated and feeling the enervating fatigue of the trek. At dawn he had squeezed the pulp of a barrelcactus through the cloth of his shirt and obtained half a pint of sour-tasting fluid. It had almost gagged him.

Logan was watching the small cleft in the yellow shale which swelled from the desert hardpan at his feet. A rattler oiled into view, tongue licking the baked air.

Logan waited, and when the snake was free of its lair, he killed it with a bootheel. Using his beltclasp, he scored the ridged skin along the back of the jaw and across the top of the broad flat head. He worked the skin loose with his teeth and pulled. It peeled smoothly back from the long body. Logan ate the pink flesh, carefully chewing the smaller bones before swallowing. The rattler joined a field mouse, three butterflies and several grasshoppers in his stomach.

He rose into the heat of the desert and went on. In theory there was a runner ahead of him who would pause to sleep. Who would falter and fall. Who would despair at the size of the desert. Because Logan did none of these he would overhaul the runner and kill him.

His tissues were pleading for water. The scant moisture provided by the snake had reawakened his water need, and the pebble in his mouth didn't help much. He remembered the class he had taken dealing with life in the desert. In the training room none of it seemed particularly difficult. The desert teemed with life, with ground owls and bats, jackrabbits and bobcats. There were gophers and mice and squirrels, foxes, badgers – and a thousand other forms crawling and slithering and inching the desert floor. But they were damned hard to trap. There was water here too, but it took luck and knowledge and instinct to find it.

His feet puffed dust in a trail that would hang in the motionless air until dusk. Then the winds would come, freezing and scouring the hardy mesquite, whipping tumbleweeds like bramble wheels on a thousand-mile journey through the arid wastes. At night the deaths would begin. Cat would stalk fox who stalked mouse who stalked insect – down through the levels of kill-to-live.

Logan stumbled and caught himself. He was tiring fast. No. A hunter does not tire. It is the quarry who tires, gives up, dies. The need for survival in a hunter must be stronger than the need of a runner, and the need of a runner is a fever in the blood.

He had to go on. He could not rest. He had to live so that runners would die.

and . . .

He was seven, and his flower had changed color and it was time to leave the nursery and go out into the world and Logan was afraid. He wanted to take Albert 6, his favorite talk puppet, with him – but they wouldn't allow it.

'Why, why, why?' he sobbed.

'Not permitted,' said his Autogoverness, and reached for Albert.

The puppet ran after Logan, tiny feet pattering across the nursery floor. 'Loge, Loge! I'll never forget you, Loge. Never forget you.'

They caught Albert and put him away in a box.

And Logan screamed and screamed and screamed.

and . . .

He was nine, and the red flower smashed against the side of his face. He was ringed by four men. The leader scowled at him. 'Lick my boot,' he said.

Logan shook his head. The man slapped him again.

'Go ahead,' said the man. 'Do it.'

He tried to back away, was shoved from behind and almost fell.

He'd been on his way to Yellowstone to meet Iron Jack who rode real horses, when they'd stopped him for no reason on the maze platform.

'Lick my boot,' said the leader. 'Then we'll let you go.'

Logan looked at the four men. He could see they ached to hurt somebody.

He bent and licked the dust from the toe of the leader's boot.

The men registered disappointment. 'Let's go,' said the leader. 'We'll find somebody with *guts.*' Then they were gone, into the maze.

I'm not going to cry, Logan told himself as his eyes blinked rapidly and the hot tears came . . .

and . . .

He was one.
He was warm.
He was clean.
He was full.

and . . .

He was thirteen, and riding the devilstick in Venice above the Piazza San Marco and the wind rushed at him and he opened his mouth to gulp the wild wine wind, and he felt the great tidal immensity of the Earth below and he was free. His palmflower was the blue of this Italian sky and it would never change and he would never grow old and it would always be clear Venice blue, Mediterranean blue and always and forever blue . . .

and . . .

I must wake. Must find Jess. Must get up.

Logan stirred in his dark metal womb. The Re-Live wall hummed.

and . . .

He was three, and the hypnotape was telling him that $A^2 + B^2 = C^2$—and of sines and cosines . . .

and . . .

He was fifteen, and the instructor bowed to him.

Logan wore the foam-padded mittens which were necessary in an Omnite class and the short white traditional shirt. He tried to do as he'd been taught, tried to clear his mind of all images except this squat, hard man before him.

'Again,' said the man.

Logan fell into the proper stance and began to circle. His hands were moist and clammy, and he fought back a desire to retreat. He must never retreat. If he wished to become a top DS operative he had to learn everything this man could teach him.

The man feinted a blow. Logan countered with a savate kick. The instructor took the impact in the belly like a stone image, without flinching, caught Logan's leg, dumped him and struck his throat, temple and solar plexus with a single continuous blow. Logan slammed the mat and was sick on the mat and the instructor said, 'There is no single blow in Omnite. Only combinations. Learn them.'

Each culture had evolved a method of personal combat. From Japan: jujitsu. From China: kempo and karate. From France: savate. From Greece: boxing and wrestling. The finest points of each art were combined in Omnite.

They circled one another. Logan struck, but was once more dumped hard to the mat. He picked himself up, wiping a thread of blood from his nose. He was stiff with pain.

'Again,' said the instructor, smiling thinly.

And again and again and again.

and . . .

He was six, and it was a play period, and Rob was scampering across the asphalt ahead of him. 'I'm a Sandman,' cried Logan. 'Here I come after ya. I see ya, Rob! You're hiding, but I see ya. I'm gonna shoot ya now!'

Logan raised the wooden Gun. Rob was behind one of the teeter-swings, pretending to be a runner.

'Bam!' yelled Logan. 'Homer! *AAAAAzzzzz*-pow!'

Rob didn't fall. 'Missed me!' he shouted.

'Did not.'

'Did too.'

'Did not. A homer never misses anybody. Ya can't get away from a homer.'

...a homer.

homer...

homer!

Up! Run! Escape!

The life drawer continued to vibrate.

Logan tensed in its metal embrace.

and...

He was nineteen, and the haunting voice sang in two-tone scale. Oh, Black, Black, B L A C K !'

He was on leave in New Alaska with a glassdancer, whose body was coated in shining scales. Outside, the forcegrown palm trees flagged the sky.

And they listened to the Cantata for Bongo in A Minor with all eighty-eight tones clear and deep from the clava drum that only Deutcher 4 could play. And there was 'Single Sung Tingle Tongue Pidge' and 'Milkbelly' and 'Angerman,' the saga of DS with its 103 choruses:

Angerman was filled with fury,
He the judge and he the jury,
Gunning runner, Gunning, Gunning,
With the quarry from him running.
Homer in the Gun!

Angerman pursuing faster,
Angerman, the angry master,
Gunning runner, Gunning, Gunning,
With the coward from him running,
Fleeing from the Gun..........

Logan felt proud to be here among his friends, in his handsome black tunic, with the glossy serpent woman caressing him in secret ways to set his blood coursing...

and...

He was fourteen, and his hand was suddenly blue. Now

he had to take on the duties of adulthood to earn his way. Yesterday all had been free for the asking because he'd been a boy, but now he was a man. But that was all right, because now he could be what he had always wanted to be.

Always . . .

and . . .

He was twenty and on the hunt. The girl had been clever, crossing the river to shake him, but now she was trapped, her back to a high board fence.

Logan walked toward her.

She clawed at the boards, breaking her nails on the rough wood, then fell, huddling at the base of the fence. He raised the Gun, fired, and the homer sang in.

Logan stood there; feeling the sick emptiness flush through him. Why had she made him do this? Why hadn't she accepted Sleep? Why had she run?

. . . run

run . . .

Run!

And he was twenty-one. Suddenly, twenty-one! And his palmflower was blinking and he was high in the threemile complex, hanging by one hand from the ledge, with Lilith laughing above him and he was in Arcade on the Table with the scalpels slicing down at him and he was in the narrow corridor with Doc charging, popsickle raised, and he was on the age-warped platform under Cathedral with the cubs, a blurred bee-drone, rushing in and the drugpad shimmering at his face and he was in brined submarine darkness in the heart of Molly as the walls quaked and Whale's steglauncher was centered on his stomach and the cold green tide was rising past his chest and he was facing Warden on the ice with the wolf circle pressing in and the wind slashing and he was in the jewel cave with Jess shackled and the great block hovering on the chute and Box coming at him with that cutting hand raised and he was scrabbling for the fallen Gun in the root grass with the golden mech eagles falling down the sky at him and he was on the granite steps in Crazy Horse with the Watchman at the bottom and Francis coming closer and Jess gone and he was lost forever in the endless, night-twisting caverns and he was watching Rutago pour the Hemodrone down Jessica's throat and the devilstick was singing under him and he was above the Lame Johnny with the king diving at him and he was in the foaming white wash of the rapids and he was soaring over the strands of dread microwire and the Loveroom had him and the entrance door was sliding closed before he could reach it and he was inching up Marye's Hill with the brass cannon roaring and Jess was gone and Francis was outside the Re-Live parlor and he was . . .

Awake!

The drawer slid open, and Logan sat up.

The robot was at the far end of the hall, tending another customer, as Logan emerged from the Re-Live bed. He did not wait, pulling off the terminals. He checked the front of the building. Francis had moved on. The way was, for the moment, clear.

A police paravane was idling at a landing stage on the next level. Logan approached the driver, a spidery man with sorrowful eyes who wore a tight-fitting lemon uniform. Logan displayed his right palm. 'Perhaps you could help me?'

'Pleased to help any citizen on Lastday,' said the lawman.

'I'm – running out of time. And I hate to waste it on belt-runs. Could I pick up a ride with you?'

'Know just how you feel, citizen. Another year or two and I'll be on Lastday myself. Where can I take you?'

'Not far.' Logan pointed off to the west. 'That wooded area beyond the battleground. I'm due to meet someone there.'

'Climb aboard.'

They rose through puffs of cannon smoke. Below, General Burnside's men were massing for another try at the slope. Muskets crackled faintly. A drum throbbed. A skirl of fife music drifted up.

The officer in yellow sighed. 'Grand sight, isn't it? Me, I always come here every year whether or not I'm on duty.

Wouldn't miss the Gala. It just inspires you to see all those brave soldiers dying for what they believed in. Gives you a sense of purpose, a sense of honor. Inspiring.'

'Yes,' said Logan.

'There were real issues to fight for then,' the officer went on. 'Liberty, freedom, justice. Now things have changed. Now everything comes to us on a platter. Man's got nothing left to fight for.'

Logan nodded.

'I envy those lads on that field. They were fighting for their *future*. And what's our future?' The officer's sad eyes grew sadder. 'Sleep. For you, tomorrow. For me, next year. I used to have religion, used to figure that there was a better place beyond Sleep. I don't know anymore. Really can't be sure. I was a Zen-Baptist for awhile, then switched to – '

'Right down there,' Logan cut in, pointing. 'On the far side of those trees.'

The paravane settled in a patch of open ground. Logan got out, waved his thanks.

'Pleased to be of service. Certain you can make it into Sleep on time?'

'I can make it.'

'I could stay in the area. Give you another ride back to – '

'No, I'll be fine.'

The officer shrugged, measured Logan with a long, penetrating policeman's stare, and took to the sky again.

The flaking maze entrance at old Fredericksburg needed paint. A flight of birds burst from cover as Logan approached. Obviously Jess was not here. But had she come and gone?

He examined the stairs. A set of heavy bootprints in the dust. DS boots.

Logan eased the Gun into his hand and padded noiselessly down the stairway. The platform was deserted. Quickly he moved to the screen control box, dismantled the scanner unit. Now the loading slot would no longer be monitored and it would be possible to get Jess into a car. *If* he could find her.

Logan returned to the surface. Had Jess understood the

location of the maze? He should have given her explicit instructions. He'd have to wait and hope she could find the place. Better to wait than chance missing her. If she were still alive – and free. If.

He settled under a sheltering overhang of trees from which he could keep the entrance under observation. A bird scolded. A squirrel frisked into the open and advanced with little flirts of its tail. The squirrel frisked closer, button eyes alert and questioning. Logan killed it with a neck snap, skinned and gutted the animal and skewered it on a green stick. Hunger was a pressure in his belly; saliva filled his mouth as he thought of the cooked meat.

He removed the four remaining shells from his Gun: needler, vapor, tangler and homer. He triggered the Gun and the resultant flash from its power pack ignited a small mound of leaves and dead branches. Feeding the smokeless fire a twig at a time, Logan roasted the squirrel and ate it.

A crunching of gravel.

He smothered the blaze and took cover. The sound of breaking twigs, of running feet in brush....

Jess emerged from the woods.

He met her at the entrance.

'Hurry,' she sobbed. 'Someone's after me.'

'DS?'

'No – ' A crash of footsteps. 'Two boys. They saw my hand.'

'Into the maze,' he said. Logan hurried her down the stairway.

'The battle . . . I was separated from you . . . thought I'd lost you . . . was afraid I couldn't get here – '

'Never mind,' he told her, 'You're here.'

The platform was still deserted.

'Washington, D.C.,' said Logan to the car which arrived at their summons.

2

He is playing them now,
circling them, watching them.
He knows their destination and is not concerned.
The Follower is beamed in, tracking them. As they move, the light dot moves with them. The black flower in the girl's hand sends out its message: she's here, here, here.
It will lead him to them.
He is no longer angry or frustrated.
He is sure of his moves, utterly calm.
The mice are in the trap.

EARLY EVENING . . .

'BARRIER, FIFTY MILES AHEAD, THE CAR WARNED, slowing itself.

'Barrier, twenty-five miles ahead,' it said.

'Barrier, five miles ahead.'

'Barrier reached. Instructions, please.'

Logan and Jess sent the car back down a tunnel.

'We walk from here,' he told her.

Ahead of them the maze was blocked by a caved-in section of rock. Part of the tunnel ceiling had collapsed, choking the area with mud and rubble. They managed to skirt the obstruction by using a narrow walkway, which led them eventually to an abandoned platform.

STANTON SQUARE

The air was moist and cloying and smelled of rot. Thick vines looped themselves across the stairway which led up to the street. At the bottom of the root-clogged landing Logan stopped short, drew in a quick breath. Bootprints. One set. Leading up.

Francis must have arrived here ahead of them.

He must be waiting up there for us, thought Logan, the Gun gripped tightly in his hand.

Waiting to kill us.

The first engagement in the Little War took place at Fifteenth and K street in front of the Sheraton Bar and Grill in the heart of Washington. For over a month young people had been pouring into the city, massing for a huge demonstration to protest the Thirty-ninth Amendment to the Constitution. Like other prohibitions before it, this Compulsory Birth Control Act was impossible to enforce, and youth had taken the stand that it was a direct infringement of their rights. Bitter resentment was directed against the two arms of Governmental enforcement, the National Council of Eugenics and the Federal Birth Study Commission. Washington had no business regulating the number of children a citizen could have. Bitterness turned to talk of rebellion.

Several test cases of the new law before the Supreme Court

had failed to advance the cause of the youthful rebels. Anger swept the ranks of the nation's young. In his State of the Union address President Curtain had stressed the severity of the food shortage, as world population spiraled toward six billion. He called upon the young to exercise self-control in this crisis. But the sight of the fat, overfed President standing in living units across the country, talking of duty and restraint, had a negative effect on his audience. And the well-known fact that Curtain had fathered nine children made a showdown inevitable.

At 9:30 p.m. Common Standard Time, on Tuesday, March 3, in the year 2000, a seventeen-year-old from Charleston, Missouri, named Tommy Lee Congdon, was holding forth outside the Sheraton Bar. With firebrand intensity he called upon his youthful listeners to follow him in a march on the White House.

'If you wanta march, why don't you damn fool kids march home to bed?' demanded a paunchy, middle-aged heckler whose name is unrecorded.

It was the wrong place, the wrong time and the wrong mode of expression. Words and blows were heatedly exchanged.

The Little War had begun.

By morning, half of Washington was in flames. Senators and congressmen were dragged in terror from their homes and hanged like criminals from trees and lampposts. The police and National Guard units were swept away in the first major wave of rioting. Buildings were set afire and explosives used. During the confusion an attendant at the Washington Zoo released the animals to save them from flames. The beasts were never recaptured.

The Army was called in and tanks were deployed on the streets radiating from the Capitol, but there were only a few older troops left to man them. The majority of the nation's armed forces were under the age of twenty-one, and their sympathies lay with the rebels. There were massive defections from all the services; abandoned uniforms were strewn along the length of Pennsylvania Avenue.

The movement swept the states. But aside from the fighting in Washington the revolution was remarkably bloodless.

Angry young people took over state capitals, county seats and city halls from coast to coast. Fearful for their lives, mayors and governors and city councilmen by the score deserted their posts, never to recover them again.

Within two weeks the reins of government lay firmly in the hands of youth. The Little War had ended.

During the rioting, Brigadier General Matthew Pope authorized the use of one vest-pocket tactical atomic bomb. It was the last act of his life, and no other nuclear weapon was used in the Little War. Ground zero for the bomb was the site of the Smithsonian Institution – and the resultant crater was thereafter known as Pope's Hole. It was a remarkably dirty bomb, and for two weeks Washington was virtually uninhabitable – until the Geiger count fell low enough for observers to re-enter the city and test the atmosphere. Already the zoo animals had begun to breed.

The next year marked the beginning of the great debates on how best to solve the population crisis.

Chaney Moon had an answer. He was sixteen and blessed with a ragged, powerful voice, glittering, hypnotic eyes and a sense of personal destiny. A crowd pleaser, with the talent to make the commonplace sound novel and the preposterous seem reasonable. As proposal followed proposal his voice rose above the others in a compelling thunder. His views found solid support. In London, at Piccadilly Circus, he adressed a chanting mob of 400,000 youngsters. In Paris, speaking flawless French, he mesmerized twice that number on the west bank of the Seine. In Berlin they embraced him; Moon was the world's savior, the new Messiah. Within six months the followers of the Chaney Moon Plan numbered in the millions. It was noted by detractors that most of his people were under fifteen, but what they lacked in maturity they made up for in fanaticism.

Five years later the Moon Plan was inaugurated and Chaney Moon, now twenty-one, proved his dedication by becoming the first to publicly embrace Sleep.

Young America accepted this bold new method of self-control, and the Thinker was programed to enforce it. Eventually all remaining older citizens were executed and the first of the giant Sleepshops went into full-time operation in Chicago. One thing the young were sure of; they would never again place their fate in the hands of an older generation.

The age of government by computer began. The maximum age limit was imposed with the new system, and the original DS units were formed.

By 2072 all the world was young.

Logan squinted up the dark stairway. He did not delude himself; he was no match for Francis. The man was brilliant and unbeatable, an enemy to fear and respect. And he was somewhere up there ahead of them, his black tunic blending into the shadows.

Angerman was filled with fury . . . homer in the Gun!

Looking at Jess, Logan felt sorrow. Behind the mask of fatigue, her face was beautiful. And she seemed so young. She'd lived a full life, yet she seemed so vulnerable and young.

He waved Jess back into the tunnel gloom. She tried to protest. He hushed her lips. Then, smoke-silent, he began ascending the stairs. At the landing he slid stomach-first against the stair riser, trying to make himself small. No sound above. He didn't expect any. Francis was a hunter; he'd wait until Logan was in his sights for a clean shot. Cautiously Logan raised his head. Still nothing.

He inched up the remaining flight of stairs, taking cover at the side of the entrance. He carefully eye-combed every inch of terrain.

A swarm of gnats descended on him, but he did nothing about them. He did not move until he was positive that each leaf was a leaf, that each tree was, in fact, a tree, that each rock was made of stone instead of flesh. Then he moved.

Logan plunged through the opening into a tangle of pulped vine, rolled several feet to come up behind the bulk of a rotting log. Again he examined each feature of the surrounding area for an oddness, a stillness too still, a movement where none should be.

Old Washington.

Jungle and jungle sounds. A monkey chattered. A macaw screamed. Somewhere in the deep brush a lion rumbled.

Logan quartered the area surrounding the maze entrance; it was a choking riot of tropical growth. Giant banyans had shot out their root systems as they rose to make a foundation for other vines, ferns, creepers. Exotic plants and flowers grew from the ripe loam-mulch next to spikethorn trees. Sword grass made it impossible to see into the jungle. It was a lush confusion of dark-green, sick-green, yellow-green. Underfoot the ground bled rivulets of water – and pond lilies broke through the scum where dragonflies hovered and darted.

He walked the area slowly. Frogs and snakes plopped and slid away at his approach. Mosquitoes swarmed angrily, biting his arms and face. He was instantly mantled in sweat, and his shirt hung in hothouse damp upon his shoulders, clinging to chest and back. His trousers were wet to the knees before he had finished reconnoitering the area.

Francis was not here.

Logan returned to the tunnel's mouth. 'Jess!' he called softly. The girl came up to join him. She looked about in wonder at the jungle.

Heat from the nuclear explosion stored in tidal salts beneath the earth was still leaching out after all these years. The furnace heat, combined with the high humidity, had created a tropical rain forest. Winter ceased to exist in Washington. The site had once been a swamp, and to swamp it had returned.

Above the trees they saw the sun-tinted dome of the Capitol Building – and it seemed, to Logan, a logical place to head for in seeking Ballard. They moved off across the square into the thick of jungle.

Insects plagued them: buffalo flies and sweat bees, legions of gnats and mites, spiders and ants. Spine trees slashed at their clothing; needles from fishtail palms lanced their skin. Twining poison vines entangled them – and the voice of the jungle was the voice of rhesus and chimp, of brush pig and plumed bird and razorback.

Then – another voice. Rattling, belching, hollow, infinitely evil: the growl of a Bengal. The jungle stilled.

'Cat,' breathed Logan. 'Big one.'

The hair rose along the back of his neck. He probed the deep scar on his left arm as he remembered the black leopard....

He'd been stalking lesser kudu at Bokov's in Nairobi. At Bokov's, the most famous of the great hunting restaurants, a man could escape the pallid food of the vending slots. He could hunt his own game with the knowledge that an expert chef stood ready to prepare a gourmet's meal from the fresh-killed animal. It wasn't easy. Bokov had prided himself on the number of predators kept on the preserve; anyone who wanted fresh game must run a proper risk to obtain it. He catered to the brave, and it was a mark of prowess to say 'I dined at Bokov's.'

Logan had paid his fee, checked out a brace of weighted hunting knives and entered the bush. He was careless, over-confident. The leopard had taken him by surprise. He remembered the black speed of it, the black savagery of it. He had almost died that afternoon....

Logan and Jess did not stir. He held the Gun, set at needler. A line of black ants marched steadily down his body from neck to elbow, making a trail of his right arm. Their home, a giant ant tree, brushed Logan's shoulder. But he did not move. Any sound at this moment and the Bengal tiger, largest of his breed, might be upon them.

The growl was closer.

'I think he's got our scent,' Logan told the girl. 'Stay behind me if he charges.'

A striped flame of yellow-and-black erupted from the high grasses. Logan fired. The needle slug buried itself in the Bengal's chest. He fired again – and a vapor cloud closed over the beast.

The big cat twisted, stunned, growling murderously. The gas drove it back into the high brush.

The growl faded behind them.

When they reached the steps of the Capitol Building Jess was staggering. Her blouse was torn in a dozen places and blood stained the cloth. Reddening welts discolored the girl's face. Logan helped her mount the crumbling steps, avoiding the heavy tap roots which had split the stone. The mosquito drone followed them inside.

The interior of the building was little better than the jungle which surrounded it: vines had woven their intricate rope patterns through the chamber. Windows were shattered; the floor was root-pocked and damp with leaf mold.

Jess slid down with her back to a section of wall. Logan slipped down beside her. They didn't have to say anything to one another. Ballard was not here. Sanctuary was still illusion and fantasy.

They closed their eyes, resting in the moist heat.

Above them: an oiled glide of mottled copper. Twenty-three feet, five inches of dense muscle and crushing coil. Anaconda. The snake was hungry. It had not been satisfied with its last meal; the young ibex and two large rats had only whetted the reptile's voracious appetite. Now its pebbled outer lids raised, and it considered the food below.

The anaconda glided down through leaf-stillness toward its dozing prey, lowering itself with shining stealth, tail anchored for leverage, gliding, lowering. . . .

Jess sighed, shifted her head to Logan's shoulder, leaned back. Through the gauze of her lashes she noted the leaf branches above. One of the branches was unlike the others. One of the branches was moving. One of the branches was –

Jess screamed.

They leaped out of the reptile's path as it struck at emptiness, coiling itself into a furious looped ball of writhing chain-mail.

'He'd solve all our problems,' said Logan as they headed for the steps. 'With him around we wouldn't *need* to find Ballard.'

There were vultures on the cornice of the Senate Building as they neared it. Four raw-necked buzzards peering down with glutenous eyes as they passed beneath. Off in the jungle, something thrashed and died. The vultures flapped into motion.

Jessica shuddered. 'Ugly,' she said. 'There's no place that's safe. Anywhere we go there'll be things waiting to kill us.'

Logan kept pushing ahead. *Ballard has to be here somewhere. I know it.*

A ripe stench of hothouse peat moss, swamp water and decaying vegetation enveloped them as they crossed a wide stretch of broken ground. Several Corinthian columns of white Georgia marble lay in their path.

They moved through tumbled ruins. Here was a medley of styles: French, Roman, Renaissance, Classic Greek – gone to rubble. A trio of Ionic piers stood miraculously upright, three smooth fingers probing the sky. Entablatures and architraves were woven with vine and creeper. Scrollwork, urns, garlands, lyres, sunburst designs emerged and disappeared in the lush growth.

They didn't hear the soft pad of feet that tracked them relentlessly. They didn't see the sun-yellow night-black beast that stalked among the fallen columns. They didn't see the Bengal with the crimson smear on its chest. . . .

The evening sky darkened over Washington. Rain began to patter down. The patter became a roar. Rain punished the jungle, beating its way into the earth.

Jessica's foot drove into thick mud as she tried to avoid a head-high growth of pampas blocking her path. Logan caught her arm, drawing her quickly back. Carefully, he parted the swamp grass. 'Cottonmouths. Nest of them.'

In the dark pool: a knotted tangle of black snake bodies, blunt heads raised from the green slime with jaws wide-spread. The inside of each gaping mouth was white and cotton-soft, except for two gleaming fangs that arched from the upper jaw in twin-curved menace.

They trudged on through the downpour.

'Ballard isn't here,' said Jess. 'He *can't* be. No one can live in this place. Do you still believe he's here?'

Logan told her the truth. 'I don't know.'

They were in a field of high veldtgrass. The old Union Station Plaza area. The rain was a solid silver sheet. Logan saw a flicker of wet gold in the grass. He tensed. 'Cat! He's back. Got our spoor.'

He drew out the Gun, checked it. A homer was useless on an animal, which meant he had only a tangler to fire at the beast.

They moved off – and behind them the stalking Bengal left its wake in the grass sea.

A single jacaranda tree rose from the veldt. Logan put his back against the grainy bark and pulled Jess to him.

The tiger padded toward them.

Above the grass, in the raingloom, a light flickered on Capitol Hill. Logan's heart leapt. 'We've found him! Ballard is up *there*! He pointed to the huge bulk of Indiana limestone looming against the sky. 'Library of Congress. I was right. I knew he'd go for high ground.'

The Bengal halted forty feet away. His yellow eyes burned from the veldtgrass. He watched the two figures, hating them.

As abruptly as it began, the rain stopped.

They edged away from the jacaranda, keeping the bole of the tree between them and the tawny cat. The grass tops discharged a chaff that itched and stung their raw faces. Jessica's breathing was ragged; she'd been pushed to the edge of physical and mental endurance.

How many others were like her? Logan wondered. Others ready to run and keep on running for life. The words of the woman on the concourse came back to him: *organized*. By Ballard? He tried to recall when he'd first heard the name. Then he knew. It was the song. One of those folkchants sung to double-guitar by dark minstrels in dim tobacco dens. Logan's nostrils were filled with nicotine odors as he remembered. . . .

He's lived a double lifetime,
And Ballard is his name.
He's lived a double lifetime.
Why can't we do the same?
Ballard's lived a double lifetime,
And never felt no shame.

Think of Ballard
Think of Ballard
Think of Ballard's name.

The cat coughed.

It was closer now, off to the left, slipping through the grass, shadowing them.

They'd have a better chance if they could reach the library. Perhaps Ballard would have his own weapon and could help them deal with the cat. Also, it would have to make its attack in the open.

The Bengal veered wide, coming in from the flank to cut them off.

'Noise,' said Logan. He began clapping his hands together. Jess followed this example. The tiger hesitated. The sudden noise startled it, diverted its course.

They reached the library steps, mounted them hurriedly. A scrabble of claws on limestone. The Bengal roared, charged. Logan swept up the Gun. The huge, muscled cat was in the air, jaws slavering wide as the Gun cracked.

The tangler caught the beast in midleap, filling its mouth and throat with metal filament mesh, webbing the great head in clock-coils of steel, wrapping a shiny cocoon over the striped body.

The cat smashed into Logan, driving him down. Logan's head struck the limestone wall, stunning him.

Doubled into a spitting ball, the tiger clawed at the mesh. Bellowing in pain and frustration, it tried to loosen the thick webbing but each convulsive movement caused the strands to constrict, work deeper into the beast's throat.

As Jess watched, helpless, the tiger thrashed closer to Logan. It had a front leg free now, and its claw scored the stone.

A tall shadow filled the doorway. Corded muscle, a lean face, a presence. Watching.

Logan shook his head dazedly. The great cat's head was inches from his, and he found himself staring into the murder-depths of the Bengal's glazing eyes. Now the free claw swung up to eviscerate the hated man-thing. Logan rolled aside. Chips of scored stone powdered his shoulder as the claw missed. He shrank back, ducking, attempting to slide along the wall away from the cat; but the tiger blocked him, trapped him in an angle between wall and balustrade. Logan kicked at the beast's head with his boot. Bone crunched; the Bengal roared in pain. Its body arched spastically. He kicked again, trying to gain room to stand.

Inner agony took the beast. Its hindquarters smashed down on Logan's left leg, pinning him. Any moment now and the claw might slice into him. . . .

The shadow figure in the doorway moved. A forty-two-year-old man faced them. His lined face held a double life-time; his hair was streaked with gray.

A legend. A myth.

A nightdream come alive.

'Ballard!' gasped Jess.

He was tall, dressed in dark blues, with a hunting longbow in one hand. Notched in the bow: a steel arrow. He did not speak. His eyes were flat and cold and unreadable.

The Bengal stirred, sobbed air, its free leg jerked. The cat focused on Logan, glared at him. A rattling growl announced its hate. Logan tried to rise, but his leg was held by the beast's weight.

'Kill it!' Jess cried to Ballard. 'Use the bow!'

The tall man shook his head.

Logan's Gun lay on the wet stone where it had fallen. Ballard moved to it, kicked the weapon over the edge of the steps.

Suddenly, with a final convulsive spasm, the cat died. One moment it was a straining mass of claw and sinew and dense-packed muscle; the next it was dead meat, growing cold.

Logan levered the inert body from his leg. Stiffly he got to his feet.

The bow followed him up, the notched arrow centered on his chest.

Jess looked accusingly at Ballard. 'You would have let it kill him.'

'Yes,' he said. His voice was deep, rasping. 'Indeed I would.'

Logan shifted his feet, moved slightly to the left. Ballard's jaw tightened. He drew back the bowstring until the feathered tip of the arrow touched his right ear.

'But he's a runner,' pleaded Jess. 'He saved my life.'

'He's also Logan 3, from DS,' said Ballard.

The bowstring tightened. Logan looked at death.

Instantly Jess launched herself; she hit Ballard's side, jolting him. Her hands came up to scratch at his face. With a hitch of one shoulder he threw her off and she tumbled to the steps.

But Logan was moving. Taking advantage of the brief scuffle, he had darted into the gloomed interior of the library. An arrow sung past him as Logan stumbled and hit the floor, sliding. He plowed forward, trying to adjust to the lack of light. He tripped again, falling heavily as a second arrow flashed past him to bury itself in the looming mass of a bookshelf.

Logan penetrated farther into the musty depths of the building. Volumes of all sizes lay in faded, disordered piles on floor and tables. Bookshelves spewed forth their contents in shredded confusion. The place smelled of dying paper and rotted bindings. Rats and lizards scuttled away from him as he rolled behind an upended tangle of shelving.

A bright beam lanced into the dark room, a pinlight spot sweeping back and across, up and down. The light found him. Logan rolled away from it, scrambled to his feet. The light followed. He ducked as a steel arrow thunked solidly into the table next to his head.

He edged back; his hand found a square, heavy book. He hefted the volume and eased around a bulk of newspaper cases. The light angled toward him. Using all of his force, he hurled the book at the light. Pages fluttered the air as the volume winged for its target. It struck Ballard; the light danced crazily.

Yet a book was no match for a hunting bow.

Logan checked the space around him for a more effective weapon, found none, began to go through his pockets as the light stalked him. His fingers touched a forgotten bulge: the Muscle pad he'd taken from the platform at Cathedral. Did he dare use it? The drug could tear him apart.

Ballard was advancing. There was nowhere to run. Logan knew he had no choice. If Muscle killed him it killed him; he'd be dead either way. He brought the pad up to his nose, squeezed it sharply and inhaled twice.

His body exploded. Fire scoured his tissues; his eyes blurred, tendons wrenched. He began shaking violently as the powerful drug took effect.

The light pinned him. Ballard raised the bow.

Logan was a dazzle of hot motion. He saw the arrow laze from the bowstring and float lightly toward him. He had all the time in the world to avoid it. He stepped aside to let it pass. He could feel a terrible pressure inside his body as he watched the arrow slide smoothly into the spine of a thick volume. Finally the pressure vanished and he relaxed, feeling his power.

With easy grace he stepped toward the tall figure silhouetted in the doorway. The figure seemed suspended there. In the time it took Logan to reach him, Ballard had moved the bow only two inches. Logan deftly plucked the weapon from the man's fingers and continued toward the square patch of light which was the outside world.

He saw Jess, a still, wide-eyed statue, hands to her mouth. He swept past her down the stairs to scoop up the Gun. The drug effect was easing; he was slowing.

He stopped. He covered Ballard with the Gun.

'Out,' he said. 'Out into the light.'

'Oh . . . Logan,' said Jess, in happy relief.

Logan could feel his heart flopping like a toad inside his chest as the drug left him. He steadied himself against the doorway as Ballard moved out into the fading sunlight.

'Tell him,' urged Jess. 'Convince him. Tell Ballard that you're a runner, just as I am.'

'But I'm not,' said Logan flatly. 'I guess I never was. Ballard was right in trying to kill me.'

All of the warmth drained out of Jessica's face. She blinked, as from a physical blow.

'Sit down,' said Logan. 'Both of you.'

Jess was shaking her head slowly, unwilling to believe what she was seeing. Ballard took her arm and they sat down on the wet stone steps.

'I'm going to kill you,' said Logan. 'I've *got* to kill you.'

Near them the great cat lay sprawled in a heap of soaked gold and black. Flies and gnats and ants had already gathered to contest the corpse. They crawled into its gaping mouth, over the ivory teeth, cloaking the tongue that lolled flaccidly, scummed the unblinking yellow eyes.

Logan said, 'There's one thing I'd like to know.' His glance flicked to Ballard's right hand, to the red flower that glowed there. 'I've seen fakes, but nothing like yours. Tattoo artists, surgeons, chemists – they've all tried to duplicate the flower, but it's tamper-proof. Yet you've lived two lifetimes and that flower is real. How? How have you gone on living?'

'One day at a time,' said Ballard with the trace of a smile.

Logan leveled the Gun.

'I'll tell you,' said Ballard. 'It won't make any difference if you know.'

Logan could not look directly at Jess, couldn't meet her eyes.

'I'm a statistical freak,' said Ballard. 'When I was born something went wrong in the nursery. The Hourglass malfunctioned, and the crystal it placed in my palm was imperfect. I didn't know this until I became twenty-one and my hand failed to blink. The flower stayed red, and I lived on while others died. . . .'

'I don't need to hear any more,' said Logan. He stepped to the edge of the steps, cupped his lips and shouted, 'Francis!' The cry echoed off into the jungle to be smothered by heat and darkness. Logan called again. 'Francis, *this* way! Here!'

He waited. Francis did not appear.

Ballard turned to Jess. 'He's a DS man. It's his life. It's what he was trained for.' He kept his voice low as Logan scanned the jungle. 'There's one consolation. He'll never find the others, the runners in Sanctuary.'

Jess looked intently at him. 'Then – there really *is* a Sanctuary, a place where people can grow old, have families, raise their own children?'

'There is.'

Logan shouted again, received no answer. He walked over to them.

'I know I could never make you tell me where Sanctuary is,' he said to Ballard. 'But after you're dead, the line will be broken.'

Ballard said nothing.

Logan brought up the Gun, set on homer. The single charge would kill them both at this range. 'Goodbye Jess,' he said softly. 'I have to do this.'

Logan pulled the trigger.

His hand was stone; the trigger finger would not move. He tried to fire, could feel muscles lock in conflict in the hand. His face went gray; the hand would not obey him. He saw Jessica's face and only Jessica's face. It was a white oval against the dark building, her eyes filled with pain and accusation.

Logan slumped back against the wall, slid down it loosely. He was making sounds. But not words. The Gun dangled limply in his hand.

Ballard stood up with Jess beside him. He took the girl aside, keeping an eye on Logan. The DS man was blind to their words and movements.

'I *knew* he could never do it,' said Jess, watching Logan with pity. 'You can trust him now.'

'Not at all,' said Ballard.

'But . . . why? After what he's – '

'Logan is a man in torment. He's in a near-trance at this point, babbling, totally exhausted. Inwardly he's torn. Half of him wants to run, escape, live. The other half wants to destroy me and you, to crush the Sanctuary line and justify his entire existence. Right now I couldn't tell you which half will win.' Ballard paused. 'You'll have to go the rest of the way alone.'

'But I love him,' protested the girl. 'You can't ask me to abandon him now.'

'Alone,' said Ballard sharply. 'Listen to me. The final stage is Cape Steinbeck and' – he checked the time – 'you've only twenty-eight minutes to get there. If you fail to make it they'll leave without you. Don't argue. You'll find a mazecar at the platform just below Capitol Hill. Now go. I'll take care of Logan.'

He turned from Jess, back to the hunched figure.

The blow which knocked him unconscious was totally unexpected.

1

He breathes deeply.
His eyes are closed.
He knows the final stage to Sanctuary.

EVENING . . .

LOGAN REACHED THE MAZE PLATFORM, NUMB, dull-eyed, one arm around Jessica's shoulder. She was guiding him, partly supporting him.

She summoned the car.

Logan's head was down; his breathing was shallow, his face flat chalk. He seemed unaware of his surroundings as the car swept into motion.

'It's going to be all right,' Jess said, holding him against her, holding him as the Loveroom had held him, talking softly to him. 'We're on the way, to the last stage, to Sanctuary. No one can stop us now. A few minutes more and we can quit running. It's all over now. It's all right. Everything's all right.'

Logan didn't respond.

The car burned through the deep tunnels.

'Listen – you don't have to fight yourself any longer. I had to keep Ballard from hurting you because what I said to him was true, about my loving you. It's not easy to discard a lifetime, but you've done it, Logan. You're free now.'

Slowly he raised his hand, his right hand. The palm flower was blinking faster.

It wavered.

It went black.

His twenty-four hours were up.

A high, keening alarm-scream rose from the car. No – from something *in* the car.

'Gun,' said Logan, trancelike. He jerked his head up, blinked rapidly as adrenalin roused him. His voice hardened. 'Wild Gun.'

'What does it mean?'

It meant a Gun in the hands of a runner, a man on black. What DS fears most. A Wild Gun. The alarm would spread in widening circles. Police units would converge. Every platform would be covered. An all-out hunt now, with DS on crash alert. The Gun was alive on every board. Dispatchers would be triangulating their position.

Logan punched the control. The car slowed.

'What are you doing?'

The car stopped; the hatch opened.

'Out,' said Logan.

They scrambled on to the platform. The Gun was screaming. Citizens scattered at the sound. They were isolated on the open platform. Logan summoned another car.

The Gun screamed.

A black tunic, moving toward them.

Through a blear-mist, Logan tried to focus on the dark figure. A thick-chested man. Killing eyes. Tight mouth.

The mazecar filled the slot behind Logan.

Too late.

The DS man's Gun came up. Centered. Homered.

An instant, frozen in time: *A homer never misses anybody . . . can't get away from a homer.*

. . . a homer.

homer . . .

homer!

The charge sung toward them.

Logan whipped up the screaming Gun. Fired.

Two projectiles moving. Two projectiles seeking heat. Two projectiles in collision.

The double explosion hammered the tunnel walls, rocked the platform, swatted Logan and Jess to the floor.

The DS man was chopped, spilled.

Dust sifted from the upper levels.

Logan pulled himself up, stumbled to the waiting car, pitched the screaming Gun inside, punched a destination: Omaha, Nebraska.

The car was gone. The alarm-scream faded, faded, died.

Another car. He justled Jess aboard. Away.

'What have we gained?' she asked.

'The Gun might throw them off,' he said.

'We're finished, aren't we?'

No reply.

They began switching cars. On the next platform a mob was smiling. A flush-faced woman pointed, 'Runners!' The crowd began to converge on them.

Away.

On the next platform, police.

On the next platform a ripper scored the metal flank of their mazecar.

'Only fifteen minutes left,' sobbed Jess. 'They'll leave without us.'

They emerged again at the next slot. A DS man was there.

Logan's thoughts raced. Young. Fresh Gunner. Not more than sixteen. Runners run. They don't attack.

Logan attacked.

Sick surprise on the young hunter's face as he was struck, groined and dropped.

Back into the maze.

'It's useless, isn't it?'

'Pittsburgh,' said Logan.

'What?'

'The steel city. No people there. Maybe a chance.'

Molybdenum
Chromium
Vanadium
Iron
Tantalum
Carbon
Aluminium
Nickel
Steel
Pittsburgh.

A great forge, a layering of bucket hoists and winches, of conveyors and gearing, punch presses, stamping machines, benders, shapers, buffers, lathes and tooling. Into its maw flowed coal and ore and electrical impulses; and out flowed uncountable metal products and hardware for a nation.

Pittsburgh: a single, automated machine, controlled by limit switches, thermocouples and programed circuits. A vibration, a decible assault, a hot-metal stench, buried in a black shrouding of smog, cinders, grit and petroleum pollution.

For more than a hundred years no man had lived in Pittsburgh; no man *could* live in Pittsburgh.

The hatch opened.

An acrid wash of fumed air blinded them, choked them. The area was veiled in black smoke.

'Blouse,' said Logan.

Jess shook her head, uncomprehending. The metal din was impossible.

He slipped off his shirt, wadded it, jammed it against his mouth. The girl nodded, did the same.

Logan got out, groped for the scanner box. He fisted the glass, shattering it. Now they could head for Steinbeck. No destination check with the box smashed. For the moment DS was blind.

He moved to the callbox to summon another car, but Jess tugged at his arm, pointing behind them. Logan spun. A maze-car was in the slot, hatch opening.

Logan grabbed the girl and backed into the pistoning smoke. Their lungs burned, eyes teared and stung. They crouched behind rotating machinery.

A man dismounted from the car. DS. A circular filtermask made his face a mystery.

He could be Francis.

The man fell into a fighting crouch and swept the platform with his Gun. Cautiously he advanced into the billowing smoke haze, stopped, bent down, examined the floor of the platform. Logan went cold. There, etched in cinder grime, were their footprints. The DS man straightened and moved toward them.

Logan led Jess deeper into the hammering metal din. He pressed her down, against a casing wall, indicating that she remain there.

The DS man was closer. Francis? Logan couldn't be sure. In height and build the man resembled him. And he moved with a veteran's sureness.

Logan stood up, let the operative catch a glimpse of him through the haze, then sprinted for an overhead conveyor. The man gave chase. Logan swung out and over a narrow channel between laboring grinders. He hung there, dropped.

Heat. Intense and deadening. Logan's hand touched metal; he winced, pulling back. The inferno of noise ate into his nerves. Each breath he took sent flame into his lungs; he could taste the grit between his teeth.

On. Deeper into the vast steel city, with the DS man in his wake.

Logan darted between a stamper and a rising hoist, caught the edge of the hoist and allowed himself to be carried upward.

A nitro charge shuddered the ground below him. The hoist stopped abruptly. Logan swung on to a metal walkway, ran along it. A ripper took out a chunk of the walk ahead of him.

He's getting my range, thought Logan. He's good, really good.

Logan clattered down a wind of steps, reached bottom, ran under a screeching cranelift, kept moving.

He'd shaken the hunter. But not for long.

A weapon. He needed a weapon . . .

He looked about wildly. Tool crib to his right. He grabbed a metal spanner, adjusted it, removed three large nuts from the face of a tramcart, stripped off a length of flexible cable. He tied the three nuts together – into an improvised bola. It would have to do.

He pulled himself up, on to a moving belt. The DS man was gliding toward him on another belt, back turned, probing the smoke curtain with his Gun. The belts moved in opposite directions, bearing great packing cases to a mile-distant chute. Logan ducked behind a case, hugged the wood, calculating.

The belts rumbled along at an even five miles an hour. Their intersect point was a gamble, but Logan would take it.

Bessemer sparks showered him from a spill of molten metal fountaining into a huge cradle. Fumes poisoned him. How close was the man? Logan kept his head down behind the crate. He counted to four. Stood up.

The DS operative was just across from him, turning in his direction. Quick!

The bola was a blur of rotating steel weights above Logan's head.

The Gun was on him, centering.

Logan released the spinning bola.

The Gun did not fire. It fell from the hand of the black-suited figure as the bola hit, wrapped and stunned the hunter. Arms pinioned to his body by the looped cable, he lost balance. The filtermask was dislodged. Not Francis.

Perhaps he screamed. In the cacaphony of cylinders and gears and pistons Logan could not tell.

The man cartwheeled down, legs wide, was deflected by a catwalk, continued his plunge into a bucket hoist, which caught his body, trundled it forward for a moment, over a pulley crest, then downward, into the chewing maw of the city.

He was gone.

Light was dying in the Florida Keys as Logan and Jess emerged at last from the maze. The western sky was a pale slate color, deepening into dusk; red streaks of cloud veined the horizon. It would be night soon.

Against this sky they saw the warehouses and storage sheds of Cape Steinbeck, spread over a flat expanse of concrete. The area was gray and lifeless.

'Sanctuary?' There was a deep disappointment in Jessica's tone.

Logan swung in a slow, wary circle. No sound. A watching silence. He knew eyes were examining them, weighing them.

They began to walk toward the buildings.

An amplified voice broke the silence. It crackled over the concrete. 'Halt! Identify yourselves.'

The two paused. Logan sighed with exhaustion. In a dead voice he said, 'Logan 3–1639.'

The girl said, 'Jessica 6–2298.'

'Password?'

'Sanctuary,' said Logan.

'You are entering a minefield. Do not proceed further. A guide will take you through.'

All of the energy had left Logan's wracked body. He was drugged with fatigue, sore in every muscle; his bones ached, and simple breathing was an effort. He could not move his legs with any precision. He shuffled, stumbled.

'Stand still!' cracked the amplified voice.

Logan stood by Jess, dazedly, as a figure detached itself from one of the shadow-draped buildings and approached them. The man slowed, walked in a weaving pattern across the flat ground.

He came up to them scowling. Hardness was stamped into his features. Hardness was in the line of his shoulders and the set of his head on his thick neck.

'Took you long enough. Now, do exactly what I tell you. There's less than seven minutes left and no time for talk. We're on the edge of the minefield. A wrong step will take your legs off. Understood?'

Logan nodded dully.

'Then follow me,' said the man.

Logan's legs were weighted. They were unyielding things which did not wish to obey him. As he followed the guide he kept losing his balance, righting himself, then almost falling again. If he fell he would be blown to pieces. Walking was impossibly difficult, one of the hardest feats he had ever been called upon to perform. Jess, too, was staggering with exhaustion.

Finally they were clear of the mined area.

They entered a long storage building, passed between high, crated objects.

Logan tried to focus his eyes on the objects. Silvery. Silvery shapes in shimmering white webbing – no, fiber packing. Numerals and letters on the sides: TITAN . . . STAR-SCRAPER . . . FALCONER. . . .

He knew what they were. Missiles. Crated and stacked and abandoned.

Again into the open.

Logan narrowed his eyes. Across an unbroken stretch of tarmac: a tall gantry, supporting a massive gleaming needle.

A passenger rocket!

Logan tried to weave a logical fabric from threads of confused thought. Cape Steinbeck, the space storage center at the tip of the Keys. A dead section. Like Cathedral. Like Molly. Like Washington. All stages on the Sanctuary line. Steinbeck, where the rockets and the missiles were mothballed when space flight was abandoned. Yet they were using a rocket – which meant that Sanctuary must be in space. But how?

Where? The planets in this solar system would not support life. The stars had never been reached. How?

'Keep moving,' said the guide.

They started toward the waiting rocket. Steam wisped from its lower stage. Frost condensed and evaporated from liquid oxygen and hydrogen stored inside, ready to be converted into raw power.

Logan felt a darkness sifting down. A darkness within himself; a darkness from the heavy sky above him; and a darkness from a man who wore it. Wore the darkness. Wore black. A tall man, coming. A hunter in the tunic of night. Angerman, the judge and jury....

At last, as Logan knew it had to be. At last – Francis.

A sense of doom and despair settled around him; the feeling was crushing, unsupportable. He had never experienced anything like it.

Jess saw the DS man, choked out a small cry.

Logan pushed her toward the guide. 'Take her. Get her aboard. I'll – try to stop him.'

The hard-faced man did not hesitate. He gripped Jessica's arm, propelled her toward the rocket. She fought to free herself. 'No, Logan! No!'

He ignored the fright and the urgency and the entreaty and the pain in her voice and he screamed silently, *Hear me, Francis. Hear me. I want to TALK to you. There's so much I have to say to you.*

A shudder rippled his body; the ground was sponge rubber; he kept sinking into it, tottering, pushing himself. He slipped to one knee, dragged his body up with clogging slowness. Dark was swimming it at him. He blinked it back.

The DS man was close now. Face set in rigid lines. Eyes cold, flat.

There was so much to say to Francis. That the world was coming apart, that it was dying, this system, this culture. That the Thinker was no longer able to hold it together. A new world would be formed. Living is better than dying, Francis. Dying young is a waste and a shame and a perversion. The young don't build. They use. The wonders of Man were achieved by the mature, the wise, who lived in this world before we did. There was an *old* Lincoln after the young one. . . .

Exhaustion hacked at Logan. His breath rattled in his throat.

Francis filled the sky. The Gun was in his hand.

Can I speak? Can I tell him? Will he listen?

Words. Sound. Logan spoke. Brokenly. In patches.

'World . . . dying . . . can't last . . . I saw . . . the dead places . . . heart of the system is . . . rotten . . . There'll be more . . . runners . . . more of them . . . You can't stop them . . . can't . . . We . . . We were wrong, Francis . . . death no answer . . . we must . . . build, not destroy . . . tired of killing . . . wrong . . . tired . . . I – I. . . .'

A roaring. A great humming roar in Logan's head. The rocket leaving without him? Let it go, then. Let it find Sanctuary. The roaring pulsed, intensified. And with it, black. A wave of running black that took him, filled his mouth and eyes. Black sound. And Francis, black in black. And the Gun. . . .

Someone was speaking. Someone was commanding him to open his eyes.

Francis stood above him. The DS man leaned over, pulled Logan up. The Gun was in its holster, the homer unfired.

Francis began to change. What was this? *Am I really conscious?* The skin, the very bones of Francis began to change; the face was being stripped away. The nose was altered, the jaw, the line of cheekbone. Francis was. . . .

Francis was Ballard!

'I couldn't tell you back in Washington,' the tall man said. 'I didn't trust you then. Even when you failed to use the Gun I didn't trust you. Now – I do.'

The logic was suddenly there for Logan. Ballard would need to disguise himself among the young in order to move about in the world. Every few years he'd need a new face, a new disguise. And what better disguise than that of a Sandman?

'I haven't been able to help too many of you,' Ballard was saying, 'because the only runners I can help are those I can reach. My organization is still a small one.'

'But – Doyle . . . back in Cathedral?'

'I gave him a key, told him to go for Sanctuary, but you were too quick for us, and the cubs got him.'

'Then – it was you, on the steps at Crazy Horse.'

Ballard nodded. 'I wanted to stop you then.'

'But how . . . how do you. . . .' Logan tried to frame questions, but his tongue would not function.

'I have only limited access to the Thinker. I control parts of the maze, the dark parts, but I'm learning more each day. The system *is* dying. The Thinker is dying. Someday you and Jess and the others will be able to come back – to a changed world. A good, strong one. I'm working for that, widening the cracks in the system, doing what I can. There are few I can trust. Mainly I have to work alone.'

'And – Sanctuary?'

Ballard was helping Logan toward the rocket. 'Argos,' he said. 'The abandoned space station near Mars. It's a small colony now, still crude, cold, hard to live on. But it's ours, Logan. Yours now. The jump for Argos is Darkside – on the Moon.'

He drew Logan, stumbling to the boarding ladder. Jess was there, waiting, tears in her eyes.

Jess . . . Jess, I love you!

Hands reached for him, gentled him aboard, fastened him into the launch seat. A crisp crackle of voices beginning the countdown. And in the final second, as the port closed, Logan saw Ballard giving last-minute instructions to the hard-faced guide who had led them through the minefield.

The port sealed itself.

A great shuddering noise possessed the rocket. Logan felt himself danced by energies and tremors; Jess was smiling at him; a weight pushed him down. He closed his eyes.

Ballard watched the tide of orange envelop the lower stage of the rocket. The needlecraft poised, rose ponderously, gaining speed as it left Earth. Faster now. A thunder – as it began its long run down the Atlantic Range, safe from the eyes of men.

Ballard turned, a tall, lonely figure blending with the night, and walked back over the cold ground.

0

The rocket was climbing on a golden flame, bound out and away for Darkside.

And *SANCTUARY*.